My life was like a snow globe. Just when I thought I had a direction… when I thought things were settled, everything turned upside down. At any point in time, I believed wholeheartedly that a series of unexpected twists and turns had led me to that moment. This moment included.

The flight to Houston had been uneventful. Uneventful considering that my fiancé's casket rode behind me. There was a curtain hanging between me and it, but I could *feel* it there.

Our pilot was Dylan Worthington, the brother of my fiancé's best friend, Conner. Both brothers flew for Skye Travels, a family company. Their company. Their planes.

Brady loved them like they were his own family.

He and Conner had been friends since they were children.

I stared out the window, hoping to distract myself from my thoughts. A man in uniform stood outside the Skye Travels terminal. Probably Conner Worthington. Conner would meet me here. Me and Brady.

BILLIONAIRE'S SECRET CRUSH

ALSO BY KATHRYN KALEIGH

Contemporary Romance
The Worthington Family

Billionaire's Unexpected Landing

Billionaire's Accidental Girlfriend

Billionaire Fallen Angel

Billionaire's Secret Crush

Billionaire's Barefoot Bride

The Heart of Christmas

The Magic of Christmas

In a One Horse Open Sleigh

A Secret Royal Christmas

An Old-Fashioned Christmas

Second Chance Kisses

Second Chance Secrets

First Time Charm

Three Broken Rules

Second Chance Destiny

Unexpected Vows

Begin Again

Love Again

Falling Again

Just Stay

Just Chance

Just Believe

Just Us

Just Once

Just Happened

Just Maybe

Just Pretend

Just Because

BILLIONAIRE'S SECRET CRUSH

THE WORTHINGTONS

KATHRYN KALEIGH

BILLIONAIRE'S SECRET CRUSH

WRITTEN IN THE WIND PREVIEW

Copyright © 2023 by Kathryn Kaleigh

All rights reserved.

Written by Kathryn Kaleigh.

Published by KST Publishing, Inc., 2023

Cover by Skyhouse24Media

www.kathrynkaleigh.com

To learn more about Kathryn Kaleigh, visit

www.kathrynkaleigh.com

Kathryn Kaleigh

1

CONNER WORTHINGTON

I tugged at the stiff collar of my white cotton dress shirt, resisted—barely—the urge to loosen the crimson and silver tie at my neck. Then I stopped myself and just stood perfectly still. Still like the thick humid air.

Heat glimmered visibly over the tarmac, in what was already turning out to be the first of one the hottest days this summer and in Texas that was saying a lot. It was only May. The heat amplified the scent of jet fuel, making it almost visible, too, in the shimmering waves.

It might be my imagination, but standing perfectly still—the sun baking my skin—seemed to make the heat more bearable. That level of bearability was relative. The only thing that really helped at all was stepping back into the air conditioning. Today that was not an option. Today I stood in the heat, keeping my body still, my mind blank.

An impressive Phenom waited several yards off to my right. I'd already done the preflight check in. The airplane was waiting and ready to go.

The constant roar of jets coming and going at the Houston airport never ended. It ebbed and flowed like anything else, but it never ended. Not even here on the western edge of the airport outside the Skye Travels private terminal

I slid my shades over my eyes and watched a little speck in the sky as it moved this way, slowly growing larger.

I knew that if I looked away, I could lose sight of it. So I kept my gaze focused on the little speck until it slowly took the shape of an airplane.

I knew the moment the wheels dropped down. Watched the plane make a wide turn as it came in for a landing from the west.

As the wheels hit the tarmac in a smooth as silk landing, I saw the splash of red that identified the plane as one of the Skye Travels fleet.

As the airplane, a medium sized jet, taxied toward the private terminal, I continued to wait. To stand perfectly still like a sentinel.

The steady roar of the air conditioning unit behind me blended with the roar of the jet as it neared. Two men riding on an empty luggage cart rumbled toward the airplane.

Most passengers had a car waiting for them.

But not today.

Today the passengers wouldn't need a car.

Today the plane brought the body of my best friend home.

And I had the worst job of all.

My job was to be here for his fiancé. To fly her wherever she wanted to go from here.

At least that was the plan as I knew it.

The last time I had seen my best friend, Brady Parker, an Air Force officer, was five months ago. I remembered it well.

The three of us—me, Grace, and Brady, had sat at the little bar across the street and drank to his promotion.

He was being shipped off to a classified location. And Grace was going with him.

They couldn't tell anyone, not even me, where they were

going, but I'd suspected Japan. Although I still didn't know for sure, I still suspected Japan.

I shifted from one foot to the other as the door opened and the stairs were lowered.

Brady had met Grace at an officer's reception just over two years ago. Brady had fallen in love instantly. I'd been there. I'd seen it happen with my own eyes.

I had made it a point to keep my distance from Grace, only seeing her when Brady was with her. It was a code my older brothers had taught me.

Grace had always seemed mysterious to me. Not only was she quiet, with eyes that missed nothing, she looked like she'd stepped out of the 1930s. Red lipstick. Wavy hair pulled back on either side left to cascade around her shoulders.

I'd never seen her when she wasn't wearing a blazer and a pencil skirt. Except for that one time I'd seen her wearing slacks with her blazer.

I fisted my hands and clenched my jaw. This would be just about the first time I had interacted with Grace without Brady's presence.

And now I was expected to spend the next few hours alone with her. Just her.

When my brother, Dylan, came to the door, I recognized his expression. Dylan had drawn the short straw on this one. No pilot wanted the be the one to fly with a casket. But now he'd done his part.

Brady would be delivered to his family. Then a military funeral. The whole nine yards. Brady would have been pleased. He lived for two things in life. The Air Force and Grace.

Dylan motioned for me to come his way.

I groaned and looked away. Nothing could be easy, could it?

2

GRACE MADISON

My life was like a snow globe. Just when I thought I had a direction… when I thought things were settled, everything turned upside down. At any point in time, I believed wholeheartedly that a series of unexpected twists and turns had led me to that moment. This moment included.

The flight to Houston had been uneventful. Uneventful considering that my fiancé's casket rode behind me. There was a curtain hanging between me and it, but I could *feel* it there.

Our pilot was Dylan Worthington, the brother of my fiancé's best friend, Conner. Both brothers flew for Skye Travels, a family company. Their company. Their planes.

Brady loved them like they were his own family.

He and Conner had been friends since they were children.

The landing was so smooth, I didn't even know we were on the ground until the plane started to slow down. Dylan was that good. He couldn't help but be good. His grandfather, Noah Worthington was considered one of the best pilots in the country. He had inherited his grandfather's genes.

I stared out the window, hoping to distract myself from my thoughts. A man in uniform stood outside the Skye Travels terminal. Probably Conner Worthington. Conner would meet me here. Me and Brady.

Sunlight glimmered across the tarmac and I braced myself for the Texas heat.

Born and bred in Texas, and I still couldn't bear the humid heat. It was unnatural. Like walking through an oven. That was one of the reasons I wouldn't have minded moving to Japan if it had worked out for Brady.

That and I was a lifelong learner. I'd already started playing around with the language. I was fairly certain I would never learn to write it though. I could recognize a couple of symbols, so I knew I would survive. But not without Brady. I wouldn't live in Japan without someone. I wasn't that brave.

As Dylan brought the plane to a stop, I slid my shades over my eyes. I hadn't cried for Brady. I had been and still was stunned, but my eyes stayed dry.

Brady worshiped the ground I walked on. He would have done anything for me and I had no doubt about that. He was one of those once in a lifetime people that I was fortunate enough to cross paths with.

I heard Dylan moving about in the cockpit. I would need to get up soon and face the next step in this nightmare.

I watched as two men drove an empty luggage cart up to the plane. The last time Brady and I had flown with Skye Travels, we'd had a car waiting for us. This time it looked like Brady got a luggage cart.

Leaning back against the leather headrest, I closed my eyes and unbuckled my seatbelt.

Dylan opened the door, letting in the hot, humid breeze that came with Texas.

I hadn't planned on coming back to Texas. At least not alone.

I dubbed it the snow globe effect.

Now my life would go back to the way it had been before

Brady or some semblance thereof. Brady had come into my life like a whirlwind and then just like that, he was gone.

I'd thought we had forever, but our forever was no more than a whisper of seconds.

I picked up my handbag and stood up, stretching muscles I'd barely moved since Dylan had picked me up at the Boston airport.

When Dylan turned and looked at me, I saw pity in his eyes. Probably just compassion, but there was a fine line. A fine line I hadn't developed the ability to discern.

I didn't want anyone's pity. I didn't have time for it.

I had a lot to do. A lot of decisions to make, none of them pleasant.

Now that Brady... his body... was back in Houston, his family would take him from here. My responsibility... my life... with him was over.

It was as it should be. He had asked me to marry him a hundred times. And I had said no... not now... a hundred times.

So I had no claim to anything related to him. A fiancé did not qualify as a widow.

In an odd way, it felt almost like it was meant to be this way.

"Ready?" Dylan asked.

I nodded and followed him to the door.

He went down first. I paused at the door—the threshold back into the life I had left behind when I met Brady.

I didn't regret it. I had learned a lot about myself. About life. About loss.

I wouldn't trade my experiences for anything and at the same time I wouldn't wish it on my worst enemy.

Conner Worthington stood at the bottom of the stairs.

Unlike his brother, Conner's expression was unreadable.

I wondered what Conner might be feeling.

He and Brady had been close. And they were young. Thirty-two. A thirty-two-year-old man was not supposed to have to bury his best friend.

I couldn't see Conner's eyes and I realized with a start that I wanted to. Needed to. For the first time in two days, I actually *felt* something.

Seeing Conner made me feel. I needed to see Conner's eyes. I needed to see how he felt. And for the first time in two days, since the officers had come to my door, I felt tears welling in my own eyes.

My life may be going back to the way it had been before I'd met Brady, but I wasn't the same.

3

CONNER — BEFORE

It was a cool late spring night. May. I was with my best friend Brady at a reception hall in downtown Houston. The room was elegantly decorated in an abundance of white flowers. Hydrangeas. Peonies. Gardenias.

White table clothes on the little round tables strategically placed around the room.

The reception room looked like a scene from a 1940s USO gathering. And according to Brady, that was the intention.

A five-piece orchestra, all dressed in black, in one corner provided background music. Big band music sure to get louder as the night progressed.

The guests were a mixture of military officers and civilians like myself. It was some kind of charity event. Brady had told me which one, but I'd been to so many charity events over the years they all blended together.

Brady only wanted me here because he didn't want to come alone. We stood on one side of the room filled with the scent of cigar smoke. A cigar bar was a rare thing these days and who knows how much pull they must have had to make that happen.

Unlike the USO, which according to all accounts did not allow alcohol, champagne flowed freely tonight.

A young lady dressed in an emerald green blazer and tight pencil skirt, wearing a little hat was coming our direction. She looked the part. I had to give them that.

"It's not so bad, huh," Brady said, looking in the girl's direction.

"Nothing to it," I said. "But you still owe me."

"I didn't think you'd let me off the hook."

"Not a chance."

Wondering just how long I was going to have to stay, I scanned the room. From the looks of things, I was the only one wondering that. Everyone else seemed to be having a grand time. Standing in little groups, talking, laughing. Formal events weren't really my scene. I preferred a pool hall and a beer.

I could do both, of course. As the grandson of the wealthy and powerful Noah Worthington, I had no choice but to be raised properly.

My gaze landed on one of the USO girl servers across the room. Like the others—I counted five altogether, this one was wearing a pencil skirt and blazer—hers was in a deep burgundy color. A little matching hat. Black stockings with a seam up the back. High heels.

She wore a smile on her bow shaped red lips as she turned. Her gaze landed square onto mine. And held.

For a moment, maybe two, maybe ten, everything else faded. It was just me and this girl in the room. In the world.

Up until that moment, I could not have said whether I believed in love at first sight or not. Now I knew. I most certainly did.

This girl, across the room, was that girl.

The one who would haunt me. The one that I would compare every other girl to from here on out. I knew it just as sure as I knew my own name. It was one of those deep, visceral, unexplainable sensations.

"Champagne?" The server who had been working this way stopped in front of us. She was dressed the same exact way as the girl across the room, but when she stepped in front of me, I felt nothing but annoyance for her. She blocked my view.

I took a champagne flute and I'm sure I murmured something appropriate to the girl.

"My name's Bree," she said. "Let me know if you need anything.

I took my champagne and stepped around her in the direction of the girl across the room.

But just like that she was gone.

4

GRACE — BEFORE

"Grace, come on. We're going to be late."

I wiped the red lipstick off my lips as I stared at myself in the mirror.

My best friend, Bree, sitting in the chair next to mine glanced over at me and took the tube of lipstick from my hands.

"No. No," she said. "You have to wear the lipstick." Bree had spent her formative years in New York and she still carried traces of the accent along with more than traces of New York attitude. "Like this."

She proceeded to glide the red lipstick across my lips. Red lipstick that had a rich heady scent that my usual box store lipstick didn't have. The lipstick smelled like rose and violet with a hint of wild raspberry. Vanilla and a fresh green crispness.

"Now do this," she said, rubbing her lips together.

I did as she said even though I felt more than a little silly.

"There," Bree said. "You look beautiful."

I looked in the mirror at my reflection. I looked like I belonged in another time. Maybe another place.

I fought the urge to flee. Bree had somehow gotten us these jobs and I couldn't let her down.

I'd make more money tonight than I would make in a month at the diner.

Bree leaned forward, handed me the tube of lipstick, and peered into my eyes.

"It's not hard," she said with a smile. "You're just serving drinks."

"I know," I clasped my hands in my lap to keep them from trembling. "I don't know why I'm so nervous."

Bree turned back to the mirror. Fussed with her hair. "Because you're used to serving eggs and burgers."

She wasn't wrong. My work at the diner was easy. All I had to do was put on a pair of white sneakers, an apron, and pull my hair into a ponytail. No one cared how I looked or how I walked.

Today I was wearing high heels, a skirt and blazer, and red lipstick.

My hair had been professionally styled.

I almost didn't recognize myself.

There were three other girls besides us wearing similar outfits. Five of us total to serve Air Force generals and other wealthy powerful people gathered in Houston.

Bree looked at me again. "Grace."

"What?"

"Smile."

I smiled, knowing it looked about as fake as could be.

Bree rolled her eyes. "Never mind. Just try to look pleasant."

Pleasant.

How was I going to look pleasant when I was worried about walking in high heels without falling on my face while carrying a tray of champagne flutes? I was already worried about staying upright and not spilling champagne all over the guests. Now I had to add looking pleasant.

"Time to go," Bree said, looking over my shoulder toward the door where the other girls were gathering to get started.

Standing, I balanced on the heels. Bree made it look so easy.

I followed her lead. Picked up one of the trays and carried it out into the stately reception area.

The room was crowded with impressively dressed military officers in their full formal uniforms. A quick glance told me there were about three men to every woman, but the women were dressed in either military dress or fancy evening gowns.

Squaring my shoulders, I imagined that I was someone else.

I was no longer a diner waitress. Not today. Today I was an elegant young lady helping out a friend. Serving drinks at the USO. That was the party's theme. I could do that. Be that person.

I may never know how, but somehow I started walking tall and steady in the heels and the smile on my lips was real as I stepped up to an officer wearing a dark blue formal dress uniform, decorated with silver epaulets and rows of metals on his chest.

With a quick smile in my direction, he took two glasses off my tray.

An announcement came over the speakers. "Be sure to thank our USO girls."

Laughter was followed by applause.

I had the oddest feeling that this was where I belonged. I might be wearing an outfit that harkened back to the 1940s, but my role was the same as theirs had been. To provide wholesome companionship to America's soldiers. Or at least serve them and their friends champagne.

I was, I decided in that moment, living in the wrong time.

And then I saw *him.*

The man watching me was not a soldier. He was wearing a black tux and stood next to a man wearing an officer's uniform.

Both of them watched me. Both handsome men. One in uniform. The other not.

But it was the man not in the uniform who caught my attention.

Bree was closer to them, so she was the one they took glasses of champagne from, but the ununiformed man kept his gaze on mine.

He was smiling at me with his eyes.

Something about him had my heart rate tripping into overtime.

Then Bree blocked my view as she stepped in front of them.

I continued to watch him out of the corner of my eye as I turned around, taking my empty tray back for a refill.

This, I decided, was going to be an interesting evening. It might even be fun after all.

5

CONNER

My most salient thought was that I needed to get Grace out of the unbearable heat.

She looked like she always did. Like she'd stepped out of the 1940s. Today she was wearing a black suit, no stockings. I hadn't seen her wear stockings since that first night at the reception two years ago. I wouldn't mind if she wore them again.

Realizing the direction my thoughts were taking, I looked over at Dylan.

"Good flight?" I asked.

"Considering," he said, holding out a hand for Grace as she reached the bottom of the stairs.

He left her there in my care while he retrieved her luggage from the airplane.

Within minutes three suitcases, two black and one red stood next to her.

"The red one is mine," she said to no one in particular.

"Whose are these?" Dylan asked, indicating the two black ones.

I couldn't see her eyes, but I knew she kept her gaze focused somewhere in the distance. "Brady's."

Dylan and I looked at each other. I felt sick.

First of all, my dead friend had twice as much luggage as his fiancé. Second of all, I didn't know what to say to her.

I was grieving for my friend, but she must be heartbroken. I cleared my throat.

"Come inside out of the heat."

She followed me without hesitation. The men were about to pull Brady's coffin from the airplane.

Good God. She had flown all the way from Japan with nothing but a coffin for company. There was something so wrong with that on so many levels I couldn't even begin to put it into words.

I pushed the back doors open and we stepped inside the Skye Travels terminal. Over the years, my family had updated the terminal. Although we still called it a back door, the doors leading out to the tarmac were now two glass doors with the red Skye Travels logo tastefully on the wall to the right of the door.

The waiting area had been moved to the first floor, leaving the second floor for offices and a captain's lounge.

Skye Travels employed about fifty pilots at any given time and they needed a place to work and relax before, after, and between flights.

I removed my shades as I walked inside. Grace did the same.

I almost wished she hadn't.

Her eyes were red beneath her dark, thick eyelashes. They glistened, but she wasn't crying. Nonetheless, I saw her bottom lip trembled just a little.

"Grace," I said.

She shook her head and turned away.

I waited a moment, giving her time. Feeling like I needed to say something, but not having a clue what that something would be.

There were no words for comfort and the sooner I accepted that, the better off I would be.

Then she turned back and searched my eyes looking for what, I didn't know.

I went with my gut and pulled her into a hug.

As I gathered her into my arms in an attempt to comfort her… for us to comfort each other, it occurred to me that I had never hugged Grace. Not once.

She had been engaged to my best friend. It would have been perfectly natural for me to have hugged her at some point.

As I felt her relax against me, I hugged her closer. Her arms went around my waist and she seemed to cling to me.

The poor girl had just undergone an unimaginable experience. Alone.

She'd had no one to lean on. No one to comfort her.

I knew how the military worked. They would be efficient and respectful.

But they would offer nothing beyond basic, hollow words of comfort.

We stood there as the seconds turned into a minute and I lost track of time.

"I'm sorry," she said, pushing back, breaking the contact.

"Please don't apologize," I said. I was the one who had hugged her. She had merely hugged me back until we were simply comforting each other.

My hands were still on her elbows. She seemed fragile. She seemed like she could use someone to help her stand.

"Grace," I said. "I have an airplane out there. Waiting. Ready to take you anywhere you want to go."

Her brow furrowed as she looked at me and her head tilted a little to the side.

"What do you mean?" she asked, her voice soft.

"I'll fly you anyplace you need to go."

She shook her head.

"Home. To your family."

She shook her head again.

"There's no charge," I said, realizing I really knew nothing about her. Whenever Brady flew with Skye Travels, we never charged him. We never charged friends. Friends fly free. She might not know that. Would have no reason to know that. Unless Brady told her. Still…

"This is home," she said.

"Houston?"

"Yes."

"You have family here?" I asked, feeling like I was sprinting to try to catch up.

"I'm from Houston," she said. At my confused expression, she added. "This is my home."

I almost asked if she was sure, but bit my tongue. The girl would know where her home was.

For some reason, I had been under the impression that she was from somewhere else. Where I don't know. Just somewhere else.

It was odd that I didn't know she was from Houston.

"I'll get a car," I said. "Drive you home."

With a renewed purpose now, I turned and started toward the elevator. Then on second thought, I turned, walking backwards. "Make yourself at home."

As I pressed the button taking me to the second floor, I wondered what was wrong with me.

Grace's dead fiancé—my best friend—was not even in the ground and all I could think about was how beautiful she looked standing there. Her red lips slightly parted, her green eyes moist.

I pressed my fingertips against my brow.

I had to pull myself together. Focus on my task.

But even then, I couldn't help feeling… happy. Happy that Grace's home was in Houston.

And perplexed that I hadn't known that.

Well, I thought, as I stepped out of the elevator.

I knew it now.

6

GRACE

I dropped into the nearest chair—a soft armchair—and blew out a breath.

The Skye Travels terminal always reminded me of a fancy living room. Several fancy living rooms all tucked together into one building.

I liked it that there was no background music. The only noises came from the constant roar of jets outside on the tarmac and in the distance coming and going from the main airport.

I had been strong for two days now. Since the men showed up at my door to tell me about the accident. I'd made decisions and arrangements. Most of them had involved his parents, but I was the one there in Japan with Brady. I was what Brady would have called "boots on the ground."

Now that I was home. Now that I was here with Conner, I didn't have to be so strong. Brady's parents would take care of everything now on Brady's end.

I could lean on Conner. Not that I would. But I *could*.

I wouldn't because if Conner knew who I really was, he might not, understandably, be so inclined to help me.

The fact that he didn't even know that I was a Houstonian, spoke volumes.

A man's best friend should at least know where his fiancé was from.

But the thing was... even Brady didn't know where I was from. Not exactly, anyway.

When I met Brady, I had left my world behind and I had become someone else.

People who talked about reinventing themselves had nothing on me.

I'd actually done it.

But now that Brady was gone, I didn't know what I would do.

Going back into my old world was not something I had considered an option. Unfortunately, it looked like that was exactly where I was headed.

I'd come from a succession of foster home placements, dumped out into the world at the tender age of eighteen.

I would have floundered, maybe crashed and burned, except for my friend, Bree. Bree had been there for me when I needed her.

But Bree was not answering her phone.

I forced myself not to panic. I would think of something.

I hated to think about using it, but I had the phone number of the shelter I'd spent some time in years ago. Mother Abigail had assured me I could return at any time for any reason.

While I was waiting for Conner, I called her. Asked if the address was the same. It was.

Conner was going to send me *home* in a car. I'd evaded his question about having family here... or anywhere.

I needed time to think. To figure things out.

Conner could and would help me, but... I didn't think my conscience would let me rely on him much at all.

I blew out a breath and ran a hand along my skirt. I had

other clothes, of course, but starting with the event two years ago where I had met Brady and Conner, I'd taken to dressing in a pencil skirt and little jacket anytime I went out. It gave me confidence and kept me from feeling like an imposter.

Brady didn't seem to pay much attention. He said he didn't care what I wore as long as I was with him.

After the event, the other girls—we were all basically the same size—had given me their outfits. I had been the only one who had taken to them. So I had my own burgundy suit and Bree's emerald green one. I had this black one, a white one, and one in a periwinkle blue.

It had been a good wardrobe start for my new life.

When Conner stepped off the elevator and smiled at me, my heart skittered and butterflies fluttered in my stomach.

I smiled back before I had time to think about it.

It was just Conner, I told myself.

I'd known Conner as long as I'd known Brady.

I had, in fact, met them the same night.

I never allowed myself to think about Conner much and this was not a good time to start.

7

CONNER — BEFORE

By the time I found the girl in the burgundy skirt and jacket, the orchestra had started playing big band music in earnest now just as I had predicted and the reception hall's USO theme came to life.

I had the odd sensation that I had been transported back to a time in America's history when everything was innocent.

I saw three other USO girls, one wearing white, one wearing black, and one wearing blue, but the one in the burgundy suit that I sought out was nowhere to be seen. People were starting to notice that I was walking around and round the reception hall.

Deciding I needed some air and even more, some perspective, I stepped out onto the balcony overlooking a verdant garden—a lush oasis in the middle of the city with blooming magnolia trees decorated with a smattering of clear lights.

The cigar smoke was stronger out here. Men had been well-trained to smoke outside and that's what they did. The music wasn't quite so loud, so I could hear myself think.

That's when I saw her. Holding an empty serving tray at her

side. Standing perfectly still, the gentle breeze tousling her hair.

Quickly covering the distance between us, lest she vanish again, I swept a lock of hair out of her face. She carried the scent of magnolia blossoms. Either that or the wind swept the scent over her. Either way, it suited her. The light floral magnolia scent with undertones of vanilla and jasmine.

"I'm not a soldier," I said. "but right now I wish I was."

"I don't mind," she said, her red lips curving into a little smile.

She had sparkling green eyes and seemed so… innocent. The role fit her perfectly. Or maybe she fit the role. Either way, I was enchanted.

"You're working," I said.

She shrugged, not answering. But the little smile on her bow shaped lips reached her eyes and I was a man sinking with no lifeline.

"What time do you get off?"

"I don't know. I guess when the party is over."

"Can I—?" My cell phone rang. It was my Grandpa Noah's ringtone. Not one I could ignore. "I'm sorry. I have to take this."

"Sure," she said.

I pulled my phone out of my pocket as I turned around. As I spoke to Grandpa, I saw the girl go back inside. Reminded myself that she was working.

"One of the pilots got into an accident," Grandpa said. "Can you fly Mr. White up to Dallas?"

"Tonight?" I asked, glancing at the champagne flute in my hand. I hadn't even tasted it.

"He's here. At the airport. I could do it, but I've got a doctor's appointment in the morning. It's an overnight trip. Up and back in the morning."

"No," I said. "Of course. I can do it. I'm downtown, so it'll take me about an hour to get there."

"See you then."

I disconnected the phone and arranged for a car to pick me up.

This evening had gone completely differently on so many levels from what I had planned.

I looked around for the girl in the burgundy suit, but she was nowhere to be found.

She had my heart.

And I didn't even know her name.

8

———

GRACE — BEFORE

After setting my serving tray down, I clasped my hands together to keep them from trembling.

I'd only spoken with the handsome stranger wearing a tux for a few minutes, but my heart raced like I had been running a mile.

Coming here tonight had been one of those spur of the moment decisions that turned out to be life altering.

I'd had one other such event, of a much larger scale, in my life when I was three years old. It was good that I couldn't remember that one.

But this one…

This event was not something I would soon forget.

Sure. I'd watched movies. I knew that there was a world outside of the one I lived in day in and day out.

But that world had always been an imaginary world for me. More like a fairy tale than a real life world I could step into.

My tray refilled with champagne flutes, I headed back out to disperse my flutes to the guests. I headed straight back to the balcony, but the handsome stranger wasn't there.

The scent of cigar smoke was strong, almost

overpowering the scent of the magnolia blossoms in the outside garden. The trees were lit by hundreds of little clear lights.

Going back inside, I continued to search for him while under the guise of circling the room, handing out champagne flutes to guests.

His friend, the soldier in uniform, intercepted me on my way back to the serving area, my empty serving tray at my side.

"Hi," he said.

"Hi. I'll back right back with more champagne," I said.

"It's okay," he said. "I just wanted to introduce myself. I'm Lieutenant Brady Parker."

"It's a pleasure to meet you, Lieutenant Parker."

He smiled as though amused. "Please. Call me Brady."

"Brady."

Brady had brown eyes and a kind smile. He was handsome, too, although I barely noticed.

"You had a friend," I said, with a glance over my shoulder, hoping that his friend in the black tux would suddenly appear. After what had been a good thirty minutes of searching, however, I was quickly losing hope.

"Yes," Brady said easily. "Conner. He had to leave. For a family matter."

"A family matter."

"I've gotten used to it," he said. "It happens a lot."

"Oh. Okay. I should probably take this tray back for a refill."

"Before you do," he said. "Will you take a few minutes? Walk with me out onto the balcony for some fresh air?"

I'd seen other girls taking breaks. Talking with soldiers. Apparently it was allowed. We were, after all, supposed to be emulating USO girls whose job was to make soldiers feel at home.

He held out a hand. "Please," he said. "I would be honored."

I had no choice, really, but to go with him.

I had to go out onto the balcony with Brady. My heart wasn't in it, but it was okay.

My life over the years had become one of doing what I had to do to survive. My dreams had started to seem futile over the years, so I hardly ever allowed them into my consciousness anymore.

I did what I had to do.

Stepping out onto the balcony with Lieutenant Brady Parker hardly seemed like a hardship.

I tucked my brief encounter with Conner into my heart for safekeeping.

9

———

CONNER

Grace was quiet on the ride leaving the airport heading to Houston.

Peter, our driver, sat quietly also, as he deftly maneuvered the limo into the traffic and headed south toward Houston.

Grace and I sat together in silence in the back seat of the limo. She wore her dark shades, hiding her eyes and I had no choice but to respect her privacy.

I had no way of knowing what she must be going through.

I was still processing Brady's death. I had more questions than anything else. Searching for answers was my way of coping.

Anytime I thought about it too much, I had to tamp down a surge of anger. Anger that Brady had gone overseas. Anger that he had been killed. Just anger about everything.

Grace was a welcome distraction in some ways. In other ways, she was a disturbing distraction.

For two years I had repressed my attraction for Grace. I had never said a word to Brady about seeing her first. It had been hard, but Brady and I had been lifelong friends. And she made him so damn happy.

After that first night, Brady had told me all about her. He had been so excited.

Even though I hadn't known her name, I didn't have to. I recognized her from the way he described her.

"She's the one," he'd said.

It figured. He and I were so close… so much alike… it just figured that he and I would fall for the same girl.

I had seen her first, but fate had taken me away that night.

Fate had taken me away and let Brady have her.

And now that Brady was gone, how could I begrudge him a single moment of happiness?

Still. That whisper of a conversation she and I had on the balcony at the reception two years ago was indelibly carved on my brain.

I remembered the flight I had taken that night.

I hadn't even known her name then, but I had known she was the one.

It had been hard after that, suppressing my feelings for her. But I had done it.

I had effectively convinced myself that she was *the one*, but not *the one* for me.

She was *the one* for Brady.

It had worked. I had stayed away. Only seeing her on occasions when she was with Brady. She was a quiet person by nature, so she had never said much.

A few times I caught her looking at me. Our gazes locked for a handful of seconds, then she would look away and the moment would be gone.

I told myself I imagined it. That she was merely being cordial. She was, after all, engaged to my best friend.

But now that Brady was out of the picture, I didn't know what to say to her. I barely even knew how to interact with her.

Cordially. That much was a given. But beyond that, I didn't know. I couldn't wrap my head around it. Right now, I just had to get her home.

After that, I would see her at Brady's funeral. If she needed anything, I would be there for her, of course. I would be expected to do no less.

But even as I told myself that, I caught a whiff of her magnolia scent and all thoughts went out of my mind.

I was swept back to that night two years ago. That night when Grace—this girl sitting next to me now—had quite simply stolen my heart.

Peter pulled up in front of a white two-story cottage in a quiet area just west of downtown. An old neighborhood. The area was shaded with old oak trees and had sidewalks settled into the ground with cracks that had settled permanently into the ground after bearing years of footsteps.

Grace bit her lip as she waited for Peter to come around and open the door.

"I'll walk you to the door," I said, reaching for my door handle.

"No," she said quickly, as though jarred out a daze. "There's no need. You've already done too much."

"I don't mind," I said. "I—"

Peter opened her door and she darted. She actually darted for the front door of the cottage with a wide front porch.

Peter quietly and methodically followed with her suitcase.

I got out and, leaning my elbows on the roof of the car, watched her reach the door. Watched her slip inside as someone discretely opened the door. Watched the door close behind her.

Peter discreetly set her suitcase down outside the door and walked back toward the car. One would think he did this kind of thing every day.

I sat back down in the backseat of the car.

Grief was different for everyone.

Maybe she had held it together as long as she could. I needed to just leave her be.

I'd done my duty as her fiancé's best friend. If she needed something else, I would be there.

The problem was, though, that as Peter navigated traffic heading back to the airport, I couldn't stop thinking about her.

10

GRACE

We reached the shelter—Mother Abigail's home. From the outside, it looked like a regular two-story house.

It was in an old established area of Houston. Lots of oak trees shading the sidewalks. People jogging and walking their dogs. The house looked like someone's normal home.

Once inside, though, passing through the living room, down the hall, it became evident that it was not just a home.

Mother Abigail's office was on the left and that led straight into the kitchen.

There were often girls sitting in the living room. Girls who needed a place to stay. Some came from abusive relationships. Some had unplanned pregnancies. A few were like me. No other place to be.

That's where I had met Bree. She had come from an abusive relationship. That was the reason why this address had to be kept with utmost discreetness. If an abuser found out where his girl was staying, he could cause trouble.

I had been careful not to act like this was anything other than a normal home with Conner and his driver.

Conner had wanted to come to the door. If he had, that would have been a violation and Mother Abigail didn't allow that without vetting him first. She was a good person—a nun—who fiercely protected her girls.

Men were only allowed under certain circumstances and then never allowed upstairs where the bedrooms were. I couldn't just bring Conner inside without her permission.

Mother Abigail had found me the job at the diner years ago and I had proven myself to be a good employee. She should have no trouble finding me another job.

I dropped onto the sofa and waited for Mother Abigail to come out of her office.

The place looked the same. Clean, worn furniture that had been donated from people like Conner's family. People who had enough to donate to the needy.

A vanilla scented candle burned on the mantle over the cold fireplace. I couldn't remember ever seeing wood in the fireplace. Mother Abigail was conservative, careful with every dime. She'd rather spend donations on baby formula or a coat for one of her girls than to build a fire and watch money going up in flames.

Right now the living room was empty. That was a relief. I really didn't feel like introducing myself or explaining myself to anyone. Not that I had to. Mother Abigail insisted that everyone respect everyone else's privacy. But still. Girls were curious creatures and befriending each other helped us get through difficult times.

Mother Abigail opened the door and came out. She smiled when she saw me and tears sprang to my eyes again.

This time I felt a single tear slip past my defenses and slide down my cheek. I swept it away. I'd been strong this far. It was just that seeing people who cared about me was overwhelming. I didn't have to bear the grief and fear alone anymore.

She held out her arms and I went into them. Safe in her arms, I cried.

I cried not only for Brady and the tragedy that had taken his young life, but I also cried because I had come full circle.

I was back where I started two years ago.

"Come with me," she said, taking me by the arm and leading me into the office. She handed me a tissue.

Wiping my eyes, I looked at her for direction. I was in a vulnerable position and I needed some time to get my feet back under me again.

"I'm not sure I can do this again," I told her. She would know what I meant. She would know I was talking about starting over with nothing.

"Don't worry, Dear," she said. "I have other plans for you."

Other plans? When Mother Abigail had plans for someone, that meant something.

Now my curiosity distracted me from my grief and guilt.

Grief for Brady and guilt that I was concerned about what would happen to me now that he was gone.

And then there was the guilt that I couldn't stop thinking about Conner Worthington.

11

CONNER

I made it a day. Almost. Until the next morning.

I woke the next morning feeling antsy. That was the only way I could describe it. I felt like I needed to do something.

The scheduler had taken me off any flights for three days out of respect for Brady's funeral. I appreciated the sentiment, but having so much time off seemed unnatural and I didn't quite know what to do with myself.

So I did what all good southerners do when faced with a situation such as this one.

Grace wasn't Brady's widow, but she was the closest thing he would ever get to one.

I stood outside the little two-story white cottage with a pecan pie balanced in one hand and a big potted ivy in the other. My hands full, I had to press the doorbell with my elbow.

While I waited, I took the time to look around. The house was well taken care of. Fresh paint. A swing on one end of the porch. Pretty pink and yellow geraniums and pansies spilled from hanging planters. It was very homey and welcoming.

A young lady wearing shorts walked past on the sidewalk, walking four dogs all at once. A dog walker. We had a teenager who did that at my high rise condo, but not for me. I didn't have any pets.

As I turned back, I caught sight of a calico kitten crouching in the window looking at me. Eyes wide. I smiled.

I had absolutely no idea what I was walking into. I didn't know anything about Grace's family. I made an assumption that this was her parents' house. It was a logical assumption. But it could be a sibling's house or it could be Grace's home.

The only thing I knew for certain was that this was not Brady's apartment. When they'd gone to Japan, he had cancelled his lease.

I shifted the pie in my hand and considered ringing the doorbell again. It was going to be another hot day. Since when had it started getting this hot in May anyway?

I stepped back a step when I heard the door lock click.

A trim middle-aged woman wearing jeans and a dress shirt opened the door and looked at me questioningly. Blocking the entrance, she kept one hand on the doorknob and one on the door frame.

"Hello," I said. "I'm Conner Worthington. I'm a friend of Grace's. Actually her fiancé's friend."

She looked past me, toward my BMW parked at the curb, then at the plant clutched against my chest. She was taking my measure, making an assessment.

"I'm Abigail," she said, stepping back and opening the door. "Come in."

I stepped inside and followed her into a living room with a well-worn, comfortable looking sofa and four armchairs. The television over the fireplace was off.

"Have a seat," Abigail said. "I'll be right back. You can set those things on the table there."

"Thank you."

I did as she said. I set the ivy and the pie on the table.

This was a little bit strange. I still didn't know who Abigail was, but she must be some relation to Grace.

I hoped Grace was home. Surely Abigail would have told me if she wasn't.

The clock over the mantle chimed the hour.

I waited. Checked my phone. Fidgeted. Walked to the window and back to my seat.

Then thirty minutes later, the clock chimed again.

I picked up the ivy. Examined the leaves. Straightened them.

"That's a lovely ivy," Grace said, sweeping into the room.

I automatically stood up. Gentlemanly behaviors had been drummed into my psyche for as long as could remember.

I almost didn't recognize her. She was wearing blue jeans and a white t-shirt. White sneakers. And her hair was pulled back in a ponytail, a few strands left to frame her face.

I stared at her a moment in admiration and awe, then held up the ivy.

"It's for you," I said.

She took it from me, her brow furrowed.

"I hope it's okay that I came," I said, feeling nervous as a schoolboy.

"Of course," she said, looking at me over the top of the ivy. "It's not really..."

She stopped. Set the ivy back down on the coffee table. "Please," she said. "Sit."

I sat back down and she sat across from me. Her face was slightly flushed and her eyes carried a serene glow to them. Acceptance. I saw acceptance there. And a deep sadness.

"I need to tell you something."

"Okay," I said, sitting forward. "What is it?"

"This isn't exactly my home," she said, keeping her voice low.

"Your family?"

She shrugged with a little noncommittal shake of her head.

"Friends?"

"It's hard to explain," she said after a moment's hesitation.

"You don't have to," I said, although I really wanted to know. But that was about my curiosity. Not about her.

"Can we just leave it at that for now," she asked. "that they're my friends?"

"Of course."

She smiled a little and locked her gaze onto mine in that way she had done so many times before when the three of us were together. Me. Grace and Brady.

But she held my gaze a moment longer this time and seemed to be searching for something.

"How are you?" I asked when she broke eye contact.

"What's this?" she asked, picking up the pecan pie, not answering.

"You know," I said. "It's that southern tradition when…" I let my voice trail off, not wanting to come right out and say anything about Brady.

"I know," she said.

Neither one of us wanted to say it.

But then her gaze met mine again.

And I knew that the conversation she and I had two years ago, before she met Brady, was sorely unresolved.

12

GRACE

I hadn't expected Conner to come back here. Certainly not today. The funeral wasn't until tomorrow. Today was just an in between day. A day without commitments, for me at least. A day to grieve. A day for family to prepare for tomorrow's funeral.

But I wasn't part of the family.

I suppose I could have insisted on being part of Brady's family. Of imposing myself on them. But that wasn't who I was.

I had, for all intents and purposes, been his girlfriend. The fact that there was a ring on my finger didn't mean all that much in this particular situation.

But Conner was here. Conner understood.

Or at least Conner thought he understood.

I had loved Brady. He had been good to me. Good for me. We had been a good couple and we would have been content. We would have had a good life together.

I knew all that and still I had not married him. I had put him off. Over and over again.

I told myself I wasn't ready. I told myself it wasn't the right time.

I told myself a lot of things.

As I sat there, looking into Conner Worthington's eyes, I admitted to myself that I had not told myself everything.

I never forgot that night I had met Conner. That evening on the balcony with the scent of magnolia blossoms wafting in on the evening breeze. The big band music streaming out from inside the reception hall.

He had affected me on a visceral level.

But I had not trusted it. In all fairness, I hadn't had time.

But I had had time with Brady. I had trusted that with Brady. Brady was safe.

Conner was anything but safe.

Two years ago, I had needed safety in my life more than I needed anything else. More than I had needed to risk my heart.

Looking back, I had been selfish. Looking back, I could see that I had wanted security. I had taken the first opportunity I had to get myself not only out of this shelter, but out of this way of life.

"I should get some plates," I said. "for the pie."

"Sure," he said. "Is it okay to go with you?"

I smiled at his question as I stood up. He obviously remembered I hadn't let him walk me to the door yesterday.

"If you want to," I said over my shoulder.

He followed quickly.

Mother Abigail's office door was closed. I knew it would be. As long as her door was closed, the downstairs level of the house looked like a regular house instead of the shelter that it was.

Mother Abigail had hesitated to let Conner inside. I knew it was against the rules. But I also knew that girls could have visitors. Trusted visitors.

She knew that if I trusted Conner, he had to be okay. She also knew that I was not from an abusive relationship, so that added even more to that trust when I said he wasn't a danger.

So I basically broke all the rules and led Conner back to the kitchen.

The rules didn't mean so much to me anymore, I realized with a bit of a start.

I scolded myself. I needed to make the rules matter if I was going to stay here.

And at the moment, I had nowhere else to go.

Everything was perfectly clean and tidy. Mother Abigail insisted on it. We were welcome to use the kitchen, but we had to clean it up afterwards.

The plates were all different colors and styles, but none of them were chipped. None of the silverware matched, but nobody cared.

I took two plates out of the cabinet and sat across the table from Conner. He had a little smile on his lips. That one that tipped up the corner of his mouth and showed in his eyes.

He was looking at me in a way that told me I had to be careful lest I found myself in a whole lot of trouble. And not from Mother Abigail.

It wouldn't be so bad, except that unlike Brady, Conner was not safe.

No, I admitted, looking into his sparkling blue eyes, Conner Worthington was about the furthest thing my heart could get from safe.

13

CONNER

The little kitchen in the back of the cottage fit the house perfectly. It looked a bit like what I imagined someone's grandmother's house could look like. Not my grandmother. Grandma Savannah lived in a mansion off Memorial Drive with a live-in housekeeper, a driver on staff, a gardener, and a cook.

But this kitchen with its clean counters with an old-fashioned coffee pot, a toaster oven, and a clean towel hanging across the sink. A little herb garden in the window. It looked cozy.

Grace filled two glasses with water, placed one in front of me, then sat across from me at a little square wooden table with four chairs. The finished was scuffed from what looked like years of use. Although there were only four chairs at the table, there were three extra chairs against the wall.

Abigail came into the kitchen as Grace deftly cut the pie into slices and placed them on our plates. I hadn't planned on actually eating any of the pie. I had planned to just drop if off and leave. Maybe talk to Grace for a moment. I hadn't really gotten that far.

But this was better. Much better than I had anticipated.

"Would you like some pie… M… Abigail?"

Abigail went straight to the sink. Filled a glass with water.

"No thank you," she said, turning and leaning against the cabinet as she drank her water and took in the scene. "You kids go ahead."

Grace winced and glanced at me as she picked up a fork. As she slid a bite of pie off her fork, I realized that she wasn't wearing lipstick. She didn't really need it anyway. Her lips were naturally dark pink.

I quickly pulled my gaze away from Grace's lips and turned my attention back to Abigail.

I wasn't sure what Abigail was looking for. And I couldn't decide if she wanted me here or not. I was detecting some ambivalence.

But then I didn't know how Abigail was related to Grace. It didn't seem appropriate to ask. So I simply picked up a fork and took a bite of pie.

It had been handmade by Grandma Savannah's personal chef. And, as always, it was excellent.

"This is really good," Grace said after taking a small bite.

"It's handmade," I said.

"I can tell," she said. "Did you make it yourself?"

"No," I said with a little smile and the way she was looking at me had me wishing that I had made it myself.

Abigail pushed off the sink. "Come see me later," she said to Grace.

Grace nodded. "I will."

I leaned forward after Abigail left and spoke softly. "She seems very stern."

Grace just smiled. "She's really very kind. Just protective."

I took another bite of pie and considered just why Abigail would be protective.

"Family?" I asked.

Grace raised an eyebrow.

"Right," I said. "We agreed to leave it at friends."

Grace nodded. "Thank you," she said.

"You don't have to thank me," I said.

She just shrugged and shoved her plate aside. She'd taken two bites of the pie.

What I didn't tell her was that I would have done anything for her. Even before. When she was engaged to Brady, I would have done anything for her. Perhaps for a slightly different reason.

Her eyes locked onto mine again.

Maybe a very different reason.

14

———————

GRACE

*A*fter we ate pie, I thanked Conner for coming by. For bringing the pie and the plant. I got the sense that he didn't want to leave.

But I stood up and walked to the door, allowing him to follow at his own pace. He followed quickly.

After I closed the door and threw the lock, I leaned against it and waited until I heard him drive off.

I had expected to see him yesterday. Had planned for it.

Today I hadn't expected to see him and I hadn't planned for it.

When Mother Abigail had sent me a message to come downstairs to her office right away, I hadn't quite known what to expect.

I'd just showered and had finished drying my hair. I wasn't expecting a guest. I was wearing jeans and a simple t-shirt.

There had been no time to change after Mother Abigail had finished reviewing the rules and expectations with me for having a guest, specifically a male guest.

I had told her who he was. Why—probably—he was here,

especially since she'd reported that he had come bearing a potted plant and a pie.

Mother Abigail knew me. It bothered me that she was so strict with me. But then, that was her job.

At any rate, I had to go to her office. And now was a good enough time to get it over with.

She probably had found a job for me already. I was well qualified and had good references. Maybe she had gotten my old job back.

I had mixed feelings about that. I didn't want to go back to my old job, much less my old life.

I knocked on the door, then opened it as she beckoned me to come inside.

Walking up to the chair next to her desk, I sat down. "Thank you," I said. "Conner and Brady were best friends."

Mother Abigail narrowed her eyes at me.

"So you said."

"They were."

"Grace," she said, looking at me. Then she straightened and shook her head. "Never mind."

I sat for a minute. I'd spent a lot of time in Mother Abigail's office. I felt at home here. I liked the view of the back yard. There were a couple of bird feeders that had been built by one of the girls who used to live here.

Mother Abigail always tried to find out a girl's interest and give her something positive to do.

"You wanted to see me," I said.

Mother Abigail clasped her hands in her lap, looking into my eyes again. It felt like she was searching my eyes, trying to figure something out.

"You're going to the funeral tomorrow?" she asked.

"I would like to," I said. "I don't have transportation."

"Don't worry about that," she said. "I'll make sure you get there even if I have to drive you myself."

I felt my eyes misting over. Once again, I was humbled by her kindness.

"Is that what you wanted to ask me?" I asked.

"Not really," she said. "But it's enough for now." She waved a hand in dismissal. "Go on. You can go on back to your room."

Typical Mother Abigail. She would get around to whatever it was she wanted when she was ready. She had a lot going on at any given moment.

I went upstairs, sat in the armchair in front of the window, and leaned my elbows on the window ledge.

I had a good view of where Conner had parked his car. When Mother Abigail had said he was here, I barely believed it.

I'd thought about him last night.

I told myself I thought about him because he had been so kind to me yesterday. I told myself that I thought about him because I was worried about his reaction to losing his best friend.

I told myself a lot of things, but I knew deep in my heart it was something else. Even now I found myself replaying his visit. Thinking about the way his eyes had locked onto mine.

And then the guilt returned.

I should not be thinking about Conner.

But, it seemed, there was nothing to be done about it.

15

CONNER

*E*veryone commented that it was a lovely funeral.

I reserved judgement. As far as I was concerned, it was one of the worst things—probably the worst thing—I had ever attended.

First of all, the scent of the mums was stifling. I didn't think I ever wanted to see another mum. And second, I had never quite understood why people wanted to call a funeral lovely. A wedding could be lovely. As hard as I tried to grasp the sentiment, I couldn't get it. A funeral could not be lovely.

I spent most of my time sitting in the chapel staring at Grace's profile. That was one good thing about wearing shades. No one knew which direction I was looking.

Brady's family had generously allowed her to sit with them. It was as it should have been. Grace had been engaged to Brady.

I didn't know why they hadn't married yet. I'm sure they had their reasons. They had never told me and I didn't ask. That was a personal thing.

Grace didn't cry. She showed no emotion whatsoever.

She stood when she was supposed to. Lowered her head when she was supposed to.

As far as I was concerned, the whole thing couldn't be over fast enough.

After it was over, finally, she left with Abigail, presumably to attend the reception at Brady's parents' house.

I went. And I looked for her.

But she didn't go.

After deciding for certain that Grace wasn't coming, I gave my respects to Brady's family, left, and drove straight back to what I had come to think of as Abigail's house.

The house didn't look like it would belong to Grace.

Besides, there was an odd dynamic between the two of them I hadn't quite figured out yet.

What I had figured out was that I needed to be near Grace.

It probably wasn't considered proper for me to go to her house after the funeral.

But it seemed appropriate to me.

Grace had been engaged to Brady and it seemed like people were having trouble remembering that or at least having trouble keeping it in mind.

I was driving myself, in my BMW sedan, so I didn't have to worry about what a driver might think about why I was going to visit Grace. To my way of thinking, if anyone needed company, it was her.

I didn't know why she hadn't gone to the reception. Maybe she was too drained. Maybe, and I hoped this wasn't the case, she wasn't welcome.

I hoped that if the situation was different and I was the one who had been killed, that my family would embrace the woman I had died loving.

The thought nearly had me making a U-turn at the next intersection. I should respect Grace's position. Respect that she might want to be alone.

Well, I decided as I kept going straight and turned down the street to the house where she was staying. Sometimes people might not know they needed social support.

That's what my Grandma would say, anyway.

So I parked my car on the side of the street and, watching a teenager jogging along the sidewalk, a big black lab at his side, checked my messages, before I turned off the motor.

I struck me then that I would never get another message from Brady. That, for the second time in a handful of minutes, had me nearly driving away, leaving Grace alone.

But then, I decided, she and I actually needed each other in a way that no one else did. We were the two people in the world who had been closest to Brady.

16

———————

GRACE

I sat in the armchair in front of my window and watched one of the neighbors jogging by with his black lab.

The jogger was a normal person from a normal home with a dog.

Wouldn't that be nice?

Someday, I told myself. Someday I would have a normal home with a dog. Maybe a cat, too, I added as Katness jumped into my lap. I'd left the door ajar since no one else was here and the cat had wandered in. Katness had lived here for longer than I had. I stroked her soft fur and scratched her ears the way she liked it.

I sat there, not thinking about anything, really. Long enough for the jogger's route to turn and he jogged back down the sidewalk on this side of the road.

That's when I saw the white BMW pulling up and parking on the side of the road beneath the old oak trees.

My heart jumped all over the place and I sat back, but not so far that I couldn't see him. Katness, sensing something, jumped down and took off. Sensitive cat.

Conner sat in the car for a few minutes and I wondered if he was going to get out or just drive away.

I wanted him to stay, of course, even though it made me incredibly nervous for him to be here.

When he got out of the car, I stepped back from the window.

As soon as I had gotten home, I changed into my jeans and a black Air Force t-shirt I had gotten what seemed like years ago.

Realizing I wasn't wearing shoes, I grabbed my white sneakers and slid them on, my hands trembling as I tied the laces.

By the time I had given my reflection a quick glance in the dresser mirror, Conner was ringing the doorbell.

No one was here to answer the door. I hurried from my bedroom, hitting the stairs at a run.

I could see Conner's shadow through the door window before I even got to the bottom of the stairs.

As I passed, the grandfather clock in the foyer chimed three times.

Opening the door, I caught my breath.

Conner turned and smiled at me.

"Are you okay?" he asked.

I put a hand on my chest. Was I?

"Yes," I said. "I just ran down the stairs."

He looked over my shoulder.

"Can I come in?" he asked.

"Of course." I stepped back, letting him inside.

Once he stepped past me, I locked the door.

"It seems like a nice neighborhood," he said, glancing at the locked door.

"It is." I shrugged. "Old habit."

"Not a bad one to have."

"Do you want to sit down?"

"Sure."

He followed me into the living room and we sat on either end of the sofa.

I pulled my feet up under me. Katness jumped up into his lap.

"Who's this?" he asked, letting her sniff his hands before she rubbed her back against his arm.

"That's Katness," I said.

"Is she your cat?"

"Not really," I said. I honestly didn't know whose cat she was. Mother Abigail took care of her, but no doubt one of the girls had brought her in at some point and left her.

It was just like Mother Abigail to keep the cat. Seemed she had a soft spot for strays.

"I looked for you at the reception."

"Oh," I said, sweeping my hair back and dropping it over my left shoulder. "I would have gone, but Abigail had to get to a meeting."

"I could have driven you," he said.

"It's okay," I said. "I probably should have gone, but..." I shrugged. How could I tell him that I really didn't want to be around anyone right now?

"How are you holding up?" he asked.

I blinked as I looked into his sparkling blue eyes. He was the first person who had asked me that.

"I'm okay," I said. "for the most part."

Except for having to live at the shelter again and not having a job again.

And being back in the same world where I started before that fateful night I had met both Conner and Brady.

17

———

CONNER

"How are you?" Grace asked.

She sat on the other end of the sofa, on her feet, like my sister, Camila would. Camila's husband was an Air Force veteran. He had made it through and home safely.

I'd never given it much thought until now, but he was lucky.

Katness was purring as I rubbed her ears.

"I've been better," I said. "But I'll be okay."

"How?" she asked. "How are you coping with it?"

I looked past Katness over to Grace. She was hugging a little pillow, looking at me with her wide, beautiful green eyes.

The sadness was still there. Sadness and something else I couldn't put a name to. There was a brightness to her eyes, but it wasn't tears.

"I guess I try not to think about it," I said, being as honest as could.

She made a face. "That works pretty well, doesn't it?"

"For now," I said. "It'll probably come back to haunt us later."

Her eyes widened. "You're probably right."

Katness left me and walked over to crawl into Grace's lap. She hugged the cat to her, burying her face in the cat's fur. Lucky cat. Right now I wanted to be Katness.

Shaking off the thought, I changed the conversation.

"So Abigail isn't here?" I asked.

"No. She's not back yet."

"Good," I said.

"Why do you say that?" Grace asked with a little smile.

"She's a little bit scary."

"Mother Abigail isn't scary," she said, then put a hand over her mouth.

"Mother Abigail?"

Grace blew out a sigh. "I guess it's time to tell you."

"Tell me what?" I asked, putting a hand along the back of the sofa to try to at least look relaxed. In truth, I had no idea what she was about to tell me and on the inside, I braced myself.

I'd met Brady's family and Abigail wasn't part of it. I was almost certain of it. Unless she was an estranged aunt or something.

"This is her house," Grace said.

"I rather figured that out."

"Oh. Well." She didn't seem to expect me to have.

Katness walked back over and climbed into my lap. She curled up, still purring, and kneaded her paws on my Armani slacks. I didn't really care, but I put my hand under her paws so she could knead it instead.

"Why do you call her Mother Abigail?"

"She's a nun."

"A—?" I had not expected that. "Why?"

"Why?" Grace repeated and she actually smiled.

My heart melted at that smile. It had been two years since I had seen her smile. It had been at the reception where we had met. Before she met Brady.

Even in all the times the three of us had been together, she hadn't really smiled, not like this. I was baffled by that and even more baffled that I was just now realizing it.

"I guess the same reason anyone would become a nun," she said.

"So you live here? With her?"

"Sort of. This is a women's shelter. I've lived here before."

She watched me carefully for any kind of reaction. I wondered if Brady had known that Grace had come from a shelter. Not that it mattered.

"So... You don't have any place else to go?"

She shook her head and lowered her eyes. They were moist again.

I wasn't about to make her talk any more about this than she already had. Not now.

The grandfather clock in the foyer chimed four times. How had it already been an hour since I had gotten here?

"Are you hungry?" I asked.

She looked up at me and I could see that she was grateful I had changed the subject.

"A little. There might be some pie left."

"Let's go get a pizza," I said, going with my first thought.

A rush of emotions washed over her face.

"I probably shouldn't," she said. "Brady..."

"You're probably right. But I'm guessing you've barely eaten anything lately."

She sighed. "You're right. I haven't been eating much."

"Katness," I said. "I hate to disturb your nap, but Grace and I have to leave the house."

"She'll stay there all day if you let her."

"I bet." I put the cat on the sofa next to me and stood up.

"You have cat hair," she said.

"I'll wear it proudly."

She smiled again.

And right then I made it my mission to make her smile as often as possible. A girl with a smile as beautiful as hers should not hide it away in grief or unhappiness.

18

GRACE

Conner held the door of his BMW open while I climbed in. He had already cooled it down by the time we got there.

It was one of those enviable things that people like Conner could do. Very valuable in this scorching heat.

Brady's car started remotely, too, but since he had a garage, he rarely used it.

Conner's car smelled clean and it was spotless.

He settled into the driver's side and smiled at me before he put on his shades.

I looked away. I didn't like it when he wore shades. I liked being able to see his eyes.

"Do you know this area?" I asked as he pulled away onto the street.

"Not really," he said. "Not at all." He tapped his GPS. "But a really good pizza place is seventeen minutes from here."

I nodded and leaned my head back against the seat.

I felt like I was being bad. I wasn't, but it still felt like it.

I wasn't wearing one of my skirts and jackets that I usually wore when I went out in public, to lunch or dinner. I wasn't even wearing lipstick.

But that was the least of it.

I was in Conner's car. Going to get a pizza with Conner.

We had just come from Brady's funeral, for God's sake.

If Abigail had been home, she probably would have advised against it.

But she hadn't been home and Conner had made a good point.

We did have to eat.

Besides. He and I needed each other.

Brady's family had each other, but neither one of us really fit in with them. They were his family. We were his friend and fiancé, respectively.

We knew a different Brady from the one they knew.

And besides, neither one of us could really talk to his family about him.

The thing was, though, we weren't talking about Brady.

We'd get to that, I assured myself.

"You were living with Brady before you left for Japan?" he asked, stopping at the stop sign and glancing over at me. I didn't see him look at me. I *felt* it.

"Yes. We didn't really expect to come back here."

"I didn't think so." He turned left and headed to the main road leading toward the northwest.

"What was it like?" he asked. "Japan?"

I straightened and opened my eyes. "How did you know it was Japan? I didn't think he told anyone."

"He didn't. Not sure how I knew. Just a feeling, I guess. Besides, he always wanted to go to Japan."

"He was fascinated by other cultures." That had probably been the one thing that worried me most about Brady. I worried that he'd find me boring after a time.

Sighing, I looked away. I didn't have to worry about that anymore.

"You're going to be okay," Conner said. "I'll take care of you."

His words struck me to the core, leaving me feeling warm. He would take care of me, of course, if I wanted him to. Because I had been engaged to his best friend. Brady would have done the same if the situation had been reversed.

It was a kind sentiment, but I wouldn't hold him to. Conner had his own life.

As he pulled onto the freeway, his phone rang.

"It's my sister," he said and answered it on his car speaker.

"Hey Conner. What are you doing?" Camila's voice came on loud and clear.

"Grace and I are going to get a pizza."

"Okay. Good." There wasn't so much as a hitch in Camila's response.

I'd met her briefly one time. I wouldn't have expected her to even remember me.

"Everything okay?" Conner asked.

I envied the closeness of the Worthington family. Having no family of my own, it was something I would never have.

"Yeah," she said. "Just calling to remind you about Grandma and Grandpa's barbecue on Sunday."

"It's in my calendar," he said, with a glance in my direction. "I'll be there."

They disconnected and Conner focused on navigating rush hour traffic.

We sat in companionable silence until we parked in the lot at an upscale pizza place.

"They cook their pizzas on real wood," he said.

"Sounds good." I tried to smile, but I was having trouble getting my lips to cooperate.

Coming here had been a mistake.

19

CONNER

"Good evening Mr. Worthington. Ma'am." I recognized the young man behind the counter. His name was Paul and, young as he was, he was the owner.

I'd stopped here, mostly for takeout, dozens of times.

"The usual to go?" he asked.

"Nah. We'd like a table."

"Very good."

We followed Paul through the restaurant to a booth on the back wall. The light was dim and only two other tables were filled.

"Here you go," Paul said. "I'll send a server shortly. And a bottle of rosé." He added over his shoulder as he walked away. He did that on purpose so I wouldn't have time to say no.

He was slick, I thought as I slid into one side of the booth and Grace slid into the other.

"Just so you know," he said. "There are no menus."

"How do we order?" she asked.

"He'll make whatever you like. Pizza or sandwiches."

A server came, bringing a bottle of wine and two glasses.

"We just got a sample crate of this wine," he said. "Paul

would like to know what you think about it." He poured an inch of wine in both our glasses.

"Happy to help," I said, looking questioningly over at Grace. She shrugged.

"It's not bad," I said, sipping the wine.

"It's pink." She lifted her glass and took a little sip. "And very sweet."

"Fruity."

She smiled.

"What do you think?"

"Doesn't beer usually go with pizza?"

"My kind of girl," I said. "You're right. But Paul... he's the owner... has ideas about making pizza artisan."

She looked blankly at me, then took another sip of wine.

"I guess he thinks artisan pizza calls for wine. I never asked."

She sat back and looked around the restaurant.

She looked calm and casual. Relaxed. She didn't look like she had just buried her fiancé.

I shook off the thought.

The job I had taken on was to bring a smile to her face, not to bring her down.

Paul popped back to our table.

"So? What do you think? You like?" He looked right at Grace.

She nodded, then her gaze slid to mine.

"We'll take it," I said.

Paul laughed. "What kind of pizza would you like?"

"What's your favorite?" I asked Grace.

"Anything with cheese."

I looked back to Paul, standing there patiently waiting in his white jacket, his hands behind his back.

"Why don't you surprise us?"

Paul grinned. "You are my favorite customer. I have an

appetizer for you first." He whirled around and headed back to the kitchen.

"Does he do everything?" she asked.

"Seems like it. I think he's going to be successful. What do you think?"

"I would have to agree," she said, her eyes locking onto mine.

Her green eyes had intrigued me since the moment I had first seen her. It was odd how things with her had come full circle. I almost felt like it was fate or destiny.

It was certainly one of those things that people would call a mixed blessing. I could spend time with Grace, but I had lost my best friend.

I still hadn't figured out how I was going to reconcile this in my own head, much less with her.

20

GRACE

Turned out that wine and pizza weren't so bad together.

Especially when the pizza was a work of art. No pepperoni and cheese here. This pizza had artichokes and tomatoes. A modified Margherita, maybe.

I had a glass of the rosé wine and Conner ending up having two glasses.

We lingered at the table. Neither of us seemed ready to leave. Once the tables started filling up, they filled up quickly and the noise level went up.

Somebody, Paul, no doubt, turned on some big band music that took me back to that night two years ago when we had first met.

It felt strange. A bit like coming around full circle.

Conner sat back and gazed into my eyes. In the dim light his eyes were a lovely shade of sparkling blue. Like a clear summer sky.

"Tell me what you thought about Japan," he said.

Sitting back, I pulled my gaze from his.

Each table and booth had a little candle burning. A real candle. Not the ones with the fuel cartridges.

It was a romantic setting and most of the customers were couples.

Apparently Conner came here a lot. Enough that he knew the owner. Enough that the owner seemed to know what he would like and felt comfortable trying a new menu item, a wine, out on him.

Paul, the owner, didn't ask about me or seem surprised that Conner had a companion. That could mean a lot of things. Conner brought a lot of girls and Paul was discreet. Or Conner rarely brought anyone here.

I gave up trying to figure it all out.

"Japan was… different. I was working on learning to read some of the language."

"I don't know if I could do that," he said. "I'm more than a little impressed."

"I was determined." I shrugged. "Besides, I like learning new things."

"What's your background?" he asked.

It was a simple question. One that a man like Conner wouldn't think twice about asking.

"I had some things happen when I was young." I took a deep breath. Reminded myself it was okay to tell Conner. I'd told Brady and he hadn't judged me.

I raised my eyes to his. "My parents were killed when I was three years old and I went into the system."

"I am so sorry," Conner said. "I didn't know."

"It's okay. I've adapted." I waited a beat. "Brady didn't tell you anything about me?"

Conner shook his head and glanced away.

"He talked about you. He talked about how much he loved you."

I felt the blush creep over my cheeks and hoped he didn't see it.

"He did. I knew he did," I said softly.

Then Conner changed the subject.

"You said you liked learning. Have you thought about what you might want to major in?"

"College?"

"Sure." He sat back. Studied me.

"I don't know. I like everything. Languages. History. Business."

He grinned at me.

"Maybe you're in a place to explore some of those options."

"Maybe," I said.

But I didn't really think so.

Mother Abigail had something in mind for me. A job of some kind.

And then I would be back to trading my time for a place to live.

But I couldn't tell Conner that. I didn't want him to know just how bad things could be in my world.

21

CONNER

hen Grace talked about learning, her eyes lit up. She had somehow missed out on that part of life. She was in her early twenties. She still had plenty of time to go to college. To have a good career.

I didn't ask her what kind of life she had come from, but I didn't have to. If she was living in a shelter, then she was merely existing.

I could take her away from that way of life.

But not today.

Today was not the day to be her knight in shining armor.

That would have to wait.

Brady had kept this side of her from me. Either that or he hadn't known. But I couldn't imagine him being engaged to someone and not knowing her background.

I had a second glass of wine, but before I did, I sent a message to my driver, Peter, to come and pick us up.

It was a rare night when I could have more than one drink. Most nights I had to refrain. Twelve hours bottle to throttle. But my personal rule was if I had a flight the next day, then no more than one drink for me. Usually not even that.

But I had no flights tomorrow. The next day I was booked out.

I wanted to know what Grace's plans were. I wanted to know her past and I wanted to know what she was thinking about for now.

But if she was like any normal person, she wouldn't know.

Brady had been killed suddenly, leaving her alone in this world.

They weren't married, so she had no widow's benefits that the military might have afforded her.

That's why she was back in the shelter.

I wasn't going to let her stay there for long.

She seemed comfortable there at the moment. Safe. And that was a good thing.

She needed that right now. A safe place with familiar people. Katness.

Once she had gotten over some of the initial shock of losing Brady, I would figure out a way to get her out of that shelter and into a normal home.

In the meantime, I needed for her to get used to me.

As the fiancé of my best friend, it was my job to take care of her. To make sure her life moved in a positive direction.

Did it matter that I would have done it anyway?

Did it matter that I would have done it two years ago if Brady hadn't snagged her first?

Maybe it mattered to some people. But at the moment, I wasn't so sure that it mattered to me.

Grace mattered to me.

Right now, going on two glasses of wine, I was going to let it go at that.

Grace glanced at her watch. "I have to be back at the shelter by seven."

"Curfew?"

"Yes. Unless we're at work."

"Well, then," I said. "We still have an hour."

She smiled at me. "You're very daring, you know."

I cocked my head at her. "No one has ever told me that."

And maybe, just maybe, no one had ever seen me quite the way Grace had.

22

GRACE

When we walked outside the restaurant at six fifteen, a limo was waiting for us in the parking lot.

I recognized the driver, Peter, as the one who had picked us up at the airport. He opened the back door and I slid inside.

A minute later, Conner slid into the other side. Even though there was a full two feet of space between us, he seemed dangerously close. So close I could *feel* him next to me.

The sun was still bright, but it dimmed as we drove beneath the trees.

We sat quietly, with just the roar of the tires on the road to break the silence.

By seven, I would be alone in my room, left to grieve my fiancé. I was not looking forward to that.

I wanted this time with Conner to last longer. To somehow stretch it out and shorten the time I would have alone with my own tortured thoughts.

"Do you have a flight tomorrow?" I asked, looking over at him.

"No," he said. "I have one more day off."

He was smiling lopsidedly at me as though we were in a normal situation. As though we had known each other and as though we hadn't buried my fiancé and his best friend today.

"One more day before everything goes back to normal," I said, looking away, out the window to watch the cars zipping past. Everyone had somewhere to go and someplace to be.

And yet Conner and I were right here. Together.

It almost, in a small, unsettling way, seemed like the past two years hadn't happened.

Even as my thoughts bumped up against that way of thinking, I stopped them. Thinking that way would be like putting a small fracture in my life. I feared that the small fracture would shatter my life like glass.

Even one wrong move and my life would shatter like sugar glass in my hands. Sugar glass would mean that my life had not been real. That it had been a pretense. Something that looked like something else.

And I couldn't allow that. I couldn't allow the past two years of Brady's life to not count for anything.

If we were right back where we started, did it mean that what happened in between dissolved into nothingness?

"You seem to be having deep thoughts," he said.

"Maybe," I said with a little smile. "But not so much."

"Do you need anything?" he asked.

I shook my head reflexively.

"Can I borrow your phone?" he asked.

"Why?" I asked while I handed him my phone.

He held it up to my face, then proceeded to enter something on my screen.

"There," he said, turning my phone back so I could see. "My name and my number. In your favorites. Call me anytime day or night."

I just looked blankly at him.

With a little shake of his head, he dialed his own number, then handed my phone back to me.

So now he had my number.

He put a hand over mine, held on tightly as we turned onto my street.

Every cell in my body reacted with that one simple touch.

My phone alarm went off. It was five 'til seven. I had exactly five minutes before Mother Abigail locked the door and whoever was left on this side of it, had to have a very compelling reason if they wanted to sleep inside.

Mother Abigail did not play when it came to being inside on time. She firmly believed that no matter what we did during the day, we needed time in the evening to relax and reflect on our day.

As Peter pulled the car up next to the house, I found myself completely agreeing with her.

"Thank you," I said. "for the pizza. I have to go."

As soon as the car stopped, I opened the door and dashed out, racing up the steps toward the door.

Mother Abigail was just stepping out of her office as I whirled in through the door.

She merely lifted an eyebrow as she continued her path to the front door. I heard the lock click into place before I heard the limo drive off.

I did not want to hear what Mother Abigail had to say.

I dashed up the stairs to my room and parked myself in front of the window. I watched the limo as Peter turned it around in the driveway and headed back the way they had come.

My heart was pounding insanely rapidly.

And I had a very good feeling that it wasn't just from the jog I had made up the stairs.

It had to do with one Conner Worthington.

Trouble.

23

———

CONNER

wo days later, I returned from what had been no more than a quick flight up to Dallas and back.

The weather was hot and clear, perfect for flying. It felt good to be back in the cockpit. I felt more like myself after having a few hours in the air to reflect on things.

I had to drop a businessman off and then pick him up in a couple of days. He went up to Dallas at least once a month.

The man's name was Steve. A seventy-year-old man who had had success late in life. He told me every time I saw him that if he'd made his money earlier, he'd be flying his own plane. But at this age, with his slowed reflexes and weakening eyesight, he believed it prudent to leave the flying to those of us who were younger and had gotten an earlier start.

I liked Steve. We had formed something of a friendship and he asked for me when he made his trips.

Some people would have gotten aggravated at Steve and called him a broke record. I believed that he told me the same thing every time we flew in order to make an impression. He wanted me to *hear* him.

And today his words resonated through my head as I went

through my prelanding checklist. I'd heard it before, but coming off the back of Brady's death, I heard his words differently.

"Don't put things off," he said. "If there's something you want to do, do it now. You can't get this time back. This day. Make sure you spend your minutes wisely. And. Don't worry about what other people think. Your life is not about them."

That last sentence had been new for Steve. He always added something new to his sentiments.

He was right. He was so right about everything.

It had been two days since I had seen Grace. It had been two seconds since I had thought about her.

I'd stayed away. I was rather proud of myself for that.

If there's something you want to do, do it now.

I lowered the plane's wheels and went in for a landing.

There was always something I wanted to do.

Doing ran in the Worthington family. It had started with Grandpa Noah. Grandpa Noah was the biggest doer I had ever known. If he thought it, he figured out how to make it happen.

Tonight, in fact, he was having a small gathering at his house. I didn't know who all was coming. I never knew. Sometimes he invited everyone, usually during holidays. And other times he would invite no more than one or two of us.

I firmly believed that he and Grandma had some kind of system to help them juggle not only their work and time together, but also the quality time they gave to each of their children and grandchildren.

All I knew was when I was invited, I went without question.

My wheels touched the runway in a smooth landing.

Don't put things off.

With Steve's words in my head, the airplane rushing to a stop beneath me, I decided what it was I wanted to do.

It might not be smart. It might not make a lot of sense to anyone other than me.

But *Don't worry about what other people think. Your life is not about them.*

Having decided, I felt better. Lighter.

I knew what I was going to do.

Now all I had to do was figure out how to make it happen.

Tonight was the night.

24

GRACE

I sat curled up in what had become my favorite armchair in front of the window of my bedroom.

With Katness curled up in my lap, I balanced the book I was reading around her.

From here I had a perfect view of the road. I watched people walking their dogs. Jogging. The neighbor watering the flowers in her yard across the street. Her yard was a burst of colors from purple to yellow to red.

Those were the things I saw. But I watched for a black limo or a white BMW.

I would have denied it to anyone else.

But I couldn't help it. I didn't even fault myself for it.

I considered Conner a friend. My only friend right now, truth be told. I hadn't been able to find Becca. If Mother Abigail knew where Becca was, she wasn't telling anyone.

I lost myself in the book I was reading for all of about three minutes before I flicked a glance toward the window.

Nothing but the wind blowing through the leaves of the oak trees lining the sidewalk. The hot Texas breeze that at least kept the air from getting stale.

I read a few more lines of the legal thriller I was reading and finally lost myself in the pages of the story.

Then I heard it. The car door slamming below.

I was reminded of what they said about watching for water to boil.

At any rate, I instantly recognized the white BMW sitting on this side of the street.

After standing for a minute, looking toward the house, Conner Worthington walked purposely up the sidewalk.

I gasped and, slamming my book closed, sat up.

Katness shot me a dirty look for waking her up and darted from the room. She was quite sensitive about being disturbed.

I stood up, my bare feet hitting the floor and pressed my forehead against the cool glass, but he was already at the door, too close for me to see him.

Even knowing he was here, I jumped when the doorbell rang.

I was not only barefoot, I was wearing a pair of old shorts and a t-shirt. I looked a mess.

But... why was he here?

"Grace," one of the girls called up the stairs. "Someone here to see you."

I wasn't supposed to have unannounced visitors.

Mother Abigail would say I was being a bad role model for the other girls. But no one seemed to care.

There were only two other girls living here right now and both of them were pretty laid back.

Mother Abigail was out, doing something with the church today as she usually did on Sundays.

I couldn't just leave Conner alone downstairs. I ran a quick brush through my hair on the way to my bedroom door and shrugged off my appearance. He wasn't here to court me. He was just here to do his best friend duty. To make sure I was being taken care of.

I went downstairs and stopped at the door to the living room. He was standing in front of the fireplace, his hands behind him. He looked like he hadn't a care in the world.

And he must not have any cares to just randomly show up here.

He turned around and looked at me.

"Hi," he said.

"Hi." My hands in my back pockets, I scrunched my toes beneath my feet.

I might have pretended not to care, but Conner was breathtakingly handsome in his pilot's uniform and I was sorely underdressed in my shorts and t-shirt.

25

CONNER

Someone was baking in the shelter's kitchen. Smelled like cookies or maybe a cake. The girl who let me in, unlike the stern and suspicious Abigail, simply asked who I was here to see and yelled up the stairs for Grace.

While I waited for her, I wandered into the living room and stood staring into the cold fireplace. It didn't look like it had ever even been used.

I heard Grace coming down the stairs and turned around when she stopped at the door.

I bit my lip to keep from grinning from ear to ear at the sight of her standing there looking at me like a deer in highlights.

She was barefoot, wearing shorts, and an oversized t-shirt halfway tucked in.

Her hair, in a total disarray framed her face.

She was utterly adorable.

"You're here," she said. There was probably a question in there somewhere.

I motioned for her to come inside and sit with me on the sofa.

She shrugged and walked over to the sofa, tucked her feet up beneath her, and looked at me with questions in her eyes.

"I had an idea," I said.

"What kind of idea?" Her naturally plump lips turning upwards in a fetchingly, innocent smile.

Steve was a brilliant man. I would thank him when I picked him up in Dallas early next week.

"My grandparents are having a dinner tonight. Come with me."

Her eyes widened. "Oh. I don't think—"

"You can't just sit here. You need to be around people."

I saw the hesitation in her eyes.

"I'm not dressed properly," she said.

I had her. She would come with me. Unable to contain it any longer, a smile broke out across my lips.

"We've got plenty of time," I said. "Go change clothes."

"What will they think?" she asked, softly.

"They will be glad to see you. They will be happy that you aren't just sitting home alone."

"Mother Abigail—"

"Don't worry about Abigail. I'll explain it to her."

"You don't understand," she said. "It's not just the going. If I'm not back by seven, the door will be locked and I won't be able to get back inside."

"Bring an overnight bag."

It seemed so simple to me, but then I was used to first of all, coming and going as I pleased and second, I was used to traveling overnight at the spur of the moment.

"I didn't just mean tonight," she said. "If I spend the night with a man, she won't let me get back inside. Ever."

"You won't be spending the night with a man," he said. "You'll be spending the night with my grandma. Savannah Worthington."

She looked at me crossways, her brow furrowed as she thought.

Girls' laughter drifted from the back toward the kitchen.

This wasn't such a bad place. It was just too restrictive.

I needed to be able to be spontaneous with Grace. Not have her under someone else's rules.

I'd talk to my Grandma tonight. After she met Grace. She knew Grace and what had happened, but I wasn't sure she'd actually met her.

I had some ideas. Ideas that Grace might not like, at least not at first.

But she would. She'd like them just fine.

The girl had run off with Brady shortly after they'd met.

She could certainly trust me.

And I wasn't even asking her to move to Japan or marry me or anything like that.

At least not yet.

26

GRACE

My hands trembled as I buttoned my white shirt. This was absolutely insane.

I was going off with Conner to have dinner with his family.

I hadn't even met Brady's family until over a month after I'd moved in with him. And we were actually dating. It was odd. I felt like they tolerated me, but I never sensed any particular affection.

And here I was. I hardly even knew Conner and I was on my way to meet his grandparents. THE Worthingtons. Noah and Savannah. I knew Noah Worthington not only through Brady, but by reputation. Noah had started Skye Travels. The premier private airline company in the country.

I was not ready for this. Conner was too convincing for his own good.

He was going to get me in trouble.

I'd known he was trouble the minute I'd laid eyes on him.

That was why I had chosen Brady. Besides, of course, that he was the one who was there. The one who pursued me.

Nonetheless, it had seemed quite simple at the time.

Brady had allowed me to be daring and safe at the same

time. Daring for leaving the safety of the shelter. Safe because Brady didn't... hadn't... given me butterflies. I had liked him. I had even loved him. But he had never made my hands tremble like they were now as I pulled on my jacket and straightened it over my skirt. This particular jacket was shorter than my usual ones. Brady had actually taken me shopping and bought me a few more modern things before we went to Japan.

I stepped into my heels and sat down at my dresser. I pulled my hair back. Studied it. Then let it drop. I'd just leave it down. It felt right. Relaxed and easy.

I had two tubes of red lipstick. One I had been given that night so long ago. The night I had met Brady and Conner. It was Dior and I only wore it on special occasions. The other one I had gotten at a drugstore for less than an hour's work.

I opened the tube of Dior and slid the red lipstick slowly across my lips, then pressed them together like Becca had taught me. The lipstick smelled like rose and violet with a hint of wild raspberry. Vanilla and a fresh green crispness.

It brought a mixture of memories and the excitement of something new, at the same time.

I smiled at my appearance.

They would say it was too early to move on.

And I wouldn't disagree.

But was it really moving on if it was more like a circle around?

I'd been attracted to Conner first.

I powdered my nose, knowing that the heat from just walking to the car would be enough to make my skin shiny.

I went to the closet and pulled out my suitcase. He said to pack an overnight bag. I didn't have an overnight bag. I only had this suitcase that held all my belongings.

I wasn't about to drag this suitcase with me to dinner with Conner.

It just seemed so... wrong... so improper.

I shoved it back in the closet and made a quick sweep of my room to make sure everything was in its place.

If I was going to get kicked out of here, at least my things would be in order.

On that thought, I dropped my Dior lipstick in my purse. Then grabbed the novel I was reading and stuffed it in there, too.

A girl had to be prepared, after all.

Squaring my shoulders, I left my room, closing the door behind me. Careful in the heels, I walked down the stairs and smiled when I saw Conner.

"Where's your bag?" he asked.

"I have everything I need in here," I lied, tapping my purse.

I was certain he would be bringing me back before curfew anyway.

It was just a dinner. It wasn't like I was running away with him.

"Grace?" One of the new girls stopped me. "There was this envelope in the kitchen with your name on it."

"What is it?" I asked, taking it from her.

"Just some old mail, I think," she said. "I almost forgot that Mother Abigail asked me to give it to you."

"Ready?" Conner asked me.

I stuffed the envelope into my purse alongside my novel and nodded.

"I'm ready," I said, with the surprising realization that I really was ready to leave here.

27

CONNER

Grace looked a little unsteady on her heels, at least to me. Maybe that was just my excuse to hold out my arm for her.

As we walked outside into the wall of heat, a little breeze whipped at her hair. Magnolia blossoms. She smelled like magnolia blossoms. Just like that night.

I opened the car door of my BMW and held her hand while she climbed inside.

As I walked around the back of my car, I whistled a happy little nonsensical tune and realized I was happy.

I was happy that Grace was coming with me to have dinner at my grandparents' house. Ridiculously happy.

Settling into the driver's seat, I looked over at her and smiled.

"Ready?" I asked.

"Ready," she said, with a little smile with those perfect bow shaped lips, but I could see nerves all over her. She was nervous.

That didn't bother me. If she was nervous, that meant she cared enough to be nervous.

"Have you met my grandparents?" I asked, attempting to set her at ease.

I didn't work, though.

"No," she said, looking away. "But Brady talked about them some. Talked about a lot of your family." She looked back at me. "You were like his family."

I swallowed thickly. Talking about Brady hadn't been where I was headed either.

"It was mutual," I said. Was Brady all we had in common?

Surely there was something else.

She rested her head back against the car seat and closed her eyes.

"Thank you," she murmured.

"For what?" I asked as I merged onto the freeway.

"For thinking about me and getting me out of the house for a few hours."

"It's my pleasure," I said. "No need to thank me."

"You had a flight today," she said.

"I did. I flew a regular client to Dallas. In a couple of days, when he's ready, I'll go back and get him."

"Have you always known you wanted to be a pilot?"

I smiled at the memory. "Since before I even understood what it meant. My grandfather had me sitting in a cockpit in his lap."

She smiled. "I envy that. Your history with your family."

"I wouldn't trade it for anything."

I changed lanes, got ready to exit.

"Have you ever just spontaneously hopped in an airplane and flown somewhere? Like hopping in the car and just driving until you see something interesting?"

"Sort of," I said. "We have to file a flight plan ahead of time."

"So you don't get to be spontaneous."

"Well… if you could go anywhere you wanted to go right now, where would it be?"

"I don't know," she said, with a little smile. "What's the most interesting place you've ever been?"

"Mackinac Island." I didn't even have to think about it. I'd been a lot of places, but that one drew me in for some reason.

"Where's that?"

"It's at the very top of northern Michigan."

"Is it really an island?"

"One of the most famous. Did you ever see the movie *Somewhere in Time*?"

"I don't think so."

"You have got to see it," I said, taking the next exit. "We'll watch it, okay?"

"Okay. What is it you like about the island?"

"Well. It's beautiful. And the only way to get there is to fly in or take a boat."

"No cars?"

"No cars are allowed on the island. At all. Only bicycles. Horses and carriages."

"People actually live there?"

"They do. A friend of the family lives there."

She took out her phone. Googled it.

"The Grand Hotel." She scrolled on her phone. "It looks amazing."

"It is. So if you said you wanted to go there, I could file a flight plan right now and we could be there in a couple of hours."

"Wow. Just like that?"

"Except that my grandparents are expecting us."

"Right." She took a deep breath and slowly let it out.

"There's no need to be nervous," I said.

"I'm not nervous."

I glanced over at her as I stopped at a traffic light. So she didn't want me to know that she was nervous.

No judgement. She was probably nervous about what

people would think about her getting out two days after Brady's funeral.

Steve's words came back to me again. *Don't worry about what other people think. Your life is not about them.*

One day I would share Steve's wisdom with her. But not today.

Right now, it was time introduce the girl of my heart to my grandparents.

Then I had to find a way to convince my grandmother to let her live with them until I could talk Grace into something more.

28

GRACE

I was lying to Conner all over the place. Not the best way to start off a relationship... friendship. Whatever this was.

It hurt my head to think about it. I was having a hard enough time keeping my thoughts going in any logical direction as it was.

He navigated the Houston traffic like he did it all the time. Like he didn't have someone driving him around half the time.

He turned onto Memorial, drove into an old established neighborhood, and pulled into a circle driveway.

The house was shaded by old oak trees, much like the trees along the street at the shelter. Here, though, there were flowers everywhere. Pinks, yellows, purples. The front yard popped with colors.

"My grandmother keeps up the flowers herself." Conner said, noticing my attention on the flowers.

"When does she have time?" I asked.

"Grandma Savannah has a way of stretching time to make it fit her instead of the other way around."

"She and I need to talk."

Conner laughed. "You're not kidding. I've been trying to understand how she does it."

"When you figure it out, let me know."

As he parked the car and looked at me with his dazzling blue eyes, I felt the nerves returning stronger than before.

I ran a hand along my skirt and took a deep breath.

"They're going to love you." Conner put his hand over mine.

I smiled. He was so very kind. It wasn't really meeting his family that had my nerves on edge. I couldn't tell him the truth. The truth that I had to be careful not to make this into something it wasn't.

Not to mistake his kindness for something else.

I was a grieving fiancé. Practically a widow.

I wasn't supposed to be feeling giddy about meeting Conner's grandparents.

As he went around the back of the car and opened my door, I refused to think about it.

Live in the moment. That was what Mother Abigail always told us when we were feeling worried about something. She usually meant something from our past, but it seemed to apply in this case, too.

Conner opened the door and I put my hand in his.

It would be so very easy to get used to this attention from Conner.

But there were so many things I didn't know. I didn't know if he had a girlfriend. I didn't know what level of obligation he felt towards Brady.

Maybe this was his way of taking care of me. Maybe he and Brady had some kind of pact that they would take care of each other's women. I'd heard of that happening and it wouldn't surprise me if that were the case with them.

According to Brady, he and Conner had been friends since they were children.

Guys could do that. It seemed harder for girls. The closest

I'd come to having a best friend was Becca and now I didn't even know where she was. And yet, I'd always gotten along with people.

My customers at the diner loved me, at least if their tips were any indication. Brady had loved me.

I didn't have a lot of experience with parents. I blamed that particular deficit in my life on not quite knowing what Brady's parents thought about me.

As we walked toward the door, Conner kept his hold on my hand. Probably worried about me and my wobbly high heels.

I was little bit worried, too.

And it was as good an excuse as any to let Conner hold my hand as we walked to his grandparents' front door.

He squeezed my hand and let go of mine to press the doorbell.

The door opened seconds later.

But neither of his grandparents answered the door.

"Good evening, Reginald," Conner said.

"Good evening, Mr. Conner." He looked over at me. "Miss Grace."

I glanced over at Conner. He leaned close and whispered.

"Reginald knows everything."

I smiled at Reginald. "It's a pleasure to meet you."

In the mere span of forty-five minutes, I had walked out of the world of the shelter and walked into this world. A world where people had chauffeurs and butlers running their homes.

The only common denominator. Conner.

And he acted like it was nothing at all.

For him, maybe it wasn't.

29

CONNER

I led Grace inside my grandparents' house. They'd lived here for as long as I had been alive.

Their home was a combination of cozy and elegant. I suppose it helped that they had a butler and a live-in housekeeper. Probably how my grandmother was able to stretch her time so effectively.

"Your grandparents are in the kitchen," Reginald told us.

"Thank you, Reginald."

Reginald vanished into the walls while we made our way toward the kitchen.

The tall grandfather clock in the foyer had been in the family for decades. Later I would tell Grace the story about it. About how it had been handed down from Grandma Savannah's mother from Alabama. It had a scar across the face between the six and seven where it had taken a bullet from a Union attack on one of our ancestor's homes.

But not right now. Right now, nerves were buzzing off of Grace.

I wanted to take her hand, but it didn't seem right. My

grandparents knew her as Brady's fiancé. And that was how it had to be for right now.

I had to give it time. Besides, my grandmother was more likely to take Grace in out respect of her grieving for Brady.

We stepped into the kitchen to the scent of something mouthwatering. Onions. Green peppers. Fresh tomatoes.

Grandma Savannah looked up from the big pot on the burner as we reached the door to the kitchen.

Grandpa Noah looked up, too. He held a large chopping knife in his hand.

They looked like any other retired couple companionably making dinner together in the kitchen.

They were nearing seventy, but didn't look a day over fifty. Maybe fifty-five.

Grandma set down her spoon and came around the counter to wrap her arms around me. She was a full head shorter than me. It was amazing that she was such a powerhouse of success.

I looked over her shoulder at Grandpa. He wasn't looking at me so much as he was affectionately watching his wife. Whenever he looked at her, there was so much love between them, it was all but visible.

She released me and, after taking Grace's hands in hers, pulled her into a hug, too.

"I'm so pleased to meet you, Grace," Grandma said, pulling her by the hand toward the kitchen table. "Sit. Conner said you were pretty, but he failed to mention that you're beautiful."

Grace actually blushed. I'd know how beautiful she was, of course. Had I mentioned anything about how pretty she was to my Grandma? Probably not. That was just her way.

"Go help your Grandpa," she told me. "Chop something."

Helpless to do anything else, I joined Grandpa at the kitchen island. But I kept my gaze on Grace.

"She'll be okay," Grandpa said. "Here. Chop this onion. It always makes my eyes hurt."

So I spent the next half hour chopping vegetables with Grandpa while Grandma and Grace conversed just out of earshot.

Grace was smiling, though, so whatever they were talking about wasn't distressing her.

As long as Grace wasn't distressed, I was okay with it.

"How was your flight today?" Grandpa asked.

"It was good."

"Steve, right?"

"That's right." How he kept everybody's schedules in his head, I would never know.

He, too, was a powerhouse. A force to be reckoned with. A man who had singlehandedly started the most successful private airline company in the country.

"Steve's a good man."

"He's very wise," I said, careful, now to keep my attention on what I was doing with the knife in my hands.

"He annoys a lot of people," Grandpa said. "But he really has good intentions."

"I agree with you completely," I said. "I actually learn a lot from him."

"What did he tell you today?" Grandpa asked.

I glanced up at him, but my gaze automatically strayed to Grace before coming back to the knife in my hands.

"He told me not to worry about what other people think."

"Sage advice," Grandpa said. "I hope you follow it."

I was doing my best to do just that.

I just had to be patient, that was all.

I reminded myself that Grandma talking with Grace was a good thing. If she got to know her, then maybe I wouldn't have such a hard time convincing her to let Grace stay here for a while.

"You're kinda smitten with that girl, aren't you?" Grandpa

asked, scraping bell peppers from the cutting board into the pot.

Startled, I nearly cut myself with the knife.

Then I remembered. Not only did Grandpa know everything about everyone in his family, he was also rumored to have quite a skill at matching people up.

But Grandpa hadn't matched us up. Fate had done it.

"Who else is coming for dinner?" I asked.

"No one," he said. "It's just the four of us."

Maybe it wasn't just fate after all.

30

———

GRACE

I knew that Savannah Worthington was a psychologist, but I hadn't thought about her also being the mother of four girls. I had not been prepared to find myself beneath her subtle, but intense scrutiny.

The kitchen and breakfast area was as big as the whole first floor of the shelter house.

Yet to be so big, it had a cozy feeling to it. The Worthingtons, I decided, had made a good life for themselves. They had worked hard and had been lucky.

Despite the large difference in their ages, Conner and his grandfather resembled each other. Not just in their lean build and good looks, but in their mannerisms and expressions.

My gaze strayed to them as I talked to Savannah.

Before I even realized I was doing it, she had me talking about the shelter and about how I had gotten away from it with Brady, but now that Brady was gone, I didn't know where else to go. And that I was relying on Mother Abigail to find me some type of employment.

"You know you can find your own work," Savannah said.

"I know. I guess living in the shelter, I thought I had to let her figure all that out."

"Grace," Savannah said, looking into my eyes. "You don't have to rely on her anymore. You have work experience. You can find something on your own. Have you thought about what you might want to do?"

"I want to go to college. Online. While I work. Maybe an office job. I don't know what to major in. I like everything. Psychology. Business. Languages." Realizing I was going on and on, I stopped myself. "I'm sorry. I'm saying too much."

"Don't worry about that," she said, leaning forward. "If you like, I can help you."

"How?" She had my complete attention now. Having Savannah Worthington's help was something I hadn't considered.

"Well." She sat back. Seemed to consider me. "There are several options. But one in particular."

I heard Conner laugh and my gaze shot toward him before I could do anything to stop it.

When I shifted my attention back to Savannah, she had a little smile on her lips.

"I'm sorry," I said. "What are you thinking about as far as options."

"I'm in need of an assistant," she said.

I looked blankly at her. I hadn't done any office work to speak of. I'd been a server at a diner and that was about it.

"I've never worked as an assistant," I said.

"But you're a hard worker. And you seem like you can learn just about anything."

I nodded. "Yes ma'am."

"There's only one condition about you working as my assistant."

"What's that?"

"My assistant needs to live here."

"Here? As in Houston?" I asked, being purposely obtuse.

"No," she said with a little smile. "Here as in my home."

I glanced around, mostly just to give myself time to comprehend what she was saying.

Big, floor to ceiling windows overlooked the backyard that somehow, even though being in the old neighborhood was huge. From here I could see a swimming pool and comfortable looking patio furniture.

Inside, the kitchen had two commercial size refrigerators, two dishwashers, and a two kitchen sinks, all laid out, somehow, in an inviting fashion.

"Your home is amazing," I said, bringing my gaze back to hers.

"Would you like a tour?" Savannah asked, her face brightening.

"Sure. I'd love that."

"Come on, then." She stood up. "Let me show you around."

This evening was absolutely nothing like what I had expected. I don't know what exactly that expectation had been, but I did know that it wasn't this.

"We'll be back in a few minutes," Savannah said to her husband and Conner as we walked past them.

Conner looked at me with questions in his eyes. I just shrugged and followed his grandmother.

31

CONNER

Sometime during the middle of dinner, the grandfather clock in the foyer chimed six times.

Grace seemed unconcerned with the time. I would have expected her to be worrying by now about getting back to the shelter. She'd said she brought everything with her for the night, but I knew she couldn't possibly have.

Her nerves seemed settled and she looked much more relaxed than she had on the drive over.

Somehow it came up during dinner that Grace had never seen and needed to watch the movie *Somewhere in Time.*

"We can watch it now, if you want to," Grandma suggested.

When Grace looked over at me, I just shrugged.

"Can I help you with the dishes?" Grace asked as we got up to go to the movie room.

"No need," Grandpa said. "Margo will take care of everything."

"You two go ahead, though," Grandma said. "We'll be along in a couple of minutes."

I led Grace upstairs to the movie room.

"I hope I'm not intruding," she said as we walked up the wide stairway. "I mean. If you had plans for the evening."

I looked at her curiously. "Being with you is my plan for the evening."

She didn't say anything, but I saw a little smile playing about her lips.

"Where do we sit?" she asked as we reached the windowless movie room.

"Anywhere," I said. "How about over here?"

We sat side by side in one corner of the big comfortable sectional.

We'd no more than sat down when a fluffy white cat jumped into her lap.

"Oh," she said. "Hi."

"This is Allie," I said. "Short for Alabama where Grandma was born and raised."

"Hi Allie. She's beautiful."

"And she'll let you love on her for days."

"I don't mind."

"You'll be covered in cat hair."

"I don't mind some cat hair."

Purring loudly, Allie curled up in her lap.

A few minutes later, Grandma and Grandpa came into the movie room, Grandpa put on the movie, and they sat down side by side on the other end of the sofa.

With the lights dim, I clasped her hand and relaxed just enough that our shoulders touched.

As the music from the movie started, she glanced up at me from beneath her lashes, giving me an overwhelming rush of emotions.

It felt right. Just so right.

It shouldn't feel right.

She wasn't my girl. She was Brady's girl.

Had been Brady's girl.

But now that Brady was gone, I wanted her to be my girl.

As the movie played out, Grace never pulled her eyes from the screen. I watched her more than I watched the movie. I'd seen it so many times I'd practically memorized it anyway.

I'd go back in time for her, I realized. I'd do anything for her. Anything at all.

I'd sacrificed those feelings for my best friend, but they had never left me. They had always been there.

She was my Makenna.

32

GRACE

*I*t was one of those rare summer nights when the temperature was actually bearable.

A soft breeze brought the scent of dozens of different flowers along with the sounds of crickets and frogs. If not for the low roar of cars on the roads, I might would have thought that we were in the country.

Even the stars seemed bright from where Conner and I sat on a swing in his grandparents' back yard.

"The movie didn't end right," I said.

"I agree it was a sad ending," Conner said.

He sat with one arm around the back of the swing, behind me, but not touching me.

He'd held my hand through the whole movie, and the movie had been halfway through before my heart rate settled back to some semblance of normal.

"Do you think he really went back in time?" I asked the question, mostly just to see how Conner would answer. I knew it was just a movie.

"Yes," he said without a hitch.

I looked over at him, into his sparkling blue eyes that always seemed to be smiling at me.

"Do you ever wish time travel was really possible?" I asked.

"Yes."

I smiled to myself. He didn't even hesitate.

"Me too," I said.

I didn't know what he was thinking about, but I was thinking about that night he and I had met.

Not that I didn't love Brady. It wasn't that. I had… did… love Brady. I would always think of him fondly.

If he had lived, he and I would have been content, happy even.

But he hadn't.

And now I had circled back around to Conner.

It was so very odd how that had worked.

It felt right. He felt right.

"Grace," he said. "I need to talk to my grandmother about you staying here for the night. Do you want to come with me?"

"I will," I said. "But you don't have to talk to her."

"I don't understand."

"She and I have already talked and I'm staying here tonight."

"How did you manage that?"

I laughed a little. "Your grandmother is scarily good at getting things out of people without them even realizing it."

"Won't disagree with that," he said.

I took a deep breath. I'd told Savannah that I would give her an answer soon. She had asked me to think about taking the job working as her full-time assistant.

The truth was, I hadn't had to think about it.

I'd known the minute she had said it that I would do it.

She would give me not only a job, but a place to live, and time to take online classes.

For all intents and purposes, Savannah Worthington was

my fairy godmother. She'd granted my every wish in one fell swoop.

Even the one that would keep me near Conner.

33

CONNER

It should have felt a little strange leaving Grace at my grandparents' house, but it didn't. It felt like everything was as it should be.

Driving home to my condo at nearly midnight, the traffic was light. I dropped my car off at the valet and waved at the concierge as I headed to the elevator that would take me to my condo on the nineteenth floor.

On second thought, I stopped by my mailbox and grabbed my mail.

When the private elevator opened up, I stepped out into my apartment.

Tossing the mail on the table next to the elevator, I went to stand at the window and looked down at the traffic flowing up and down the 610 freeway. It wasn't heavy, but it was steady enough. Everyone had somewhere to go.

It was baffling that out of millions of people, I had found the girl of my heart.

I would take Steve's advice and not care what anyone else thought.

It didn't matter if anyone thought it was too soon for me to begin thinking of Grace as my girl.

I would need to take her out. To dinner. To movies. Museums.

She deserved no less.

And, I thought, as I leaned against the cool floor to ceiling glass wall, I needed to give her time.

She was going to be living with my grandparents. She would be right there. I didn't have to worry about losing touch with her.

But most importantly, I didn't have to worry about her living in a shelter with strangers.

Tomorrow I would go with her and take her to get her clothes and things. To essentially move her into my grandparents' house.

Then I could start courting her.

I already knew that she was the one for me.

I didn't know how I would have dealt with it if Brady had lived. No. That was wrong. I did know.

I would have accepted it and moved on. And I would have always considered Brady the luckiest man alive.

Another girl would have come along. Someone I could love. Someone I could spend my life with and be content.

But not now. Now I didn't have to do that. Now I had everything I ever could have imagined.

On my way to my bedroom, I stopped and glanced through the mail. I didn't get much mail anymore. Everything was digital.

There was a small envelope, though, that caught my attention. Handwritten. And it hit me in the gut when I recognized the handwriting.

It was from Brady.

Fingers shaking, I sliced it open with the letter opener.

Brady had sent me a letter and I was just now getting it? I

tried to remember the last time I had checked my mail, but I couldn't put my finger on it.

Would have been at least a week. Couldn't remember checking it since I'd heard the news of Brady's accident.

Taking the letter out of the envelope, I walked over to my sofa and sat down.

I took a deep breath and began to read.

Dear Conner,

I instructed my commander to deliver this letter to you upon my death. So since you're reading this, then I've died.

I was going to be sick.

Leaving the letter on the sofa, I managed to make it to the restroom first.

34

GRACE

The cat, Allie, slept on the pillow next to mine all night. She was still there when I woke the next morning.

Waking when I did, she stood up and stretched.

"Are you my new best friend?" I asked.

Allie blinked her big blue eyes and stretched out her front legs.

"Thank you for watching over me."

Allie got up and went to stand in front of the door, swishing her tail.

"See you later," I said as she took off down the hall after I opened the door to let her out.

I'd slept in a t-shirt that Savannah had given me. A blue Skye Travels t-shirt.

I felt like I was quickly becoming a part of the family.

It was an exhilarating feeling, but it didn't come without its guilt.

I was supposed to still be grieving for Brady.

I went to the window and looked down over the east side of

the house. The morning sun glittered over the flowers still moist with morning dew.

It was hard for me to believe that I was here.

Mother Abigail would be so...

I turned and looked at the room that would be mine now while I worked for Savannah. It was twice as big as my room at the shelter. It had a four-poster bed draped with some kind of gauzy material. There was a dresser and a desk. A walk-in closet.

I didn't know what Mother Abigail would be, but she would surely be happy for me. She wanted us to all find our own success. I had found my success. Had landed on my feet after one of the worst things that a person could experience.

Yes. She would be happy for me, I decided.

It was early, too early to go downstairs, so I sat down on my bed and pulled the manila envelope of mail from my purse.

I'd assumed it was mail that arrived for me while I was in Japan. Mail Mother Abigail had saved for me. No one would know that was back living there now.

The letter was handwritten and I immediately recognized the handwriting.

Brady?

How had—?

Hands trembling, I pulled the letter out of the envelope and, sitting down on the edge of the bed, began to read.

Dear Grace,

This is about the fifth time I've started this letter.

As you must can surmise, I'm writing it with a lot of hesitancy. And honestly only because my commander insisted.

It's something he insists we do before going on a dangerous mission like the one coming up next week.

I have a surprise for you.

I should probably go ahead and tell you about it.

I stopped reading and dropped the letter into my lap. A business card fell out from the folded pages onto the bed.

Picking it up, I stared at the card. A business card for an attorney in Houston.

Without even reading the rest of the letter, I set it all on the nightstand. It was more than I could handle right now.

I sat very still, staring at the letter with suspicion and wariness. My mind was going in a million different directions.

With a sigh, I picked up the letter and started reading again from the beginning.

35

CONNER

By the time I got back from my flight the next day, it was rush hour.

I had my car at the airport and could have easily driven myself. But since I had some business to take care of, I arranged for Peter to drive me home.

It was just as well. We ended up sitting in freeway traffic, giving me plenty of time to make some phone calls.

In his last letter to me, Brady had left me the name and phone number of an attorney in Houston.

Brady expected me to take care of Grace. And by taking care of her, he asked me for one last thing.

He asked me to make sure she took what he had left behind for her.

Grace is proud and independent. She'll try to give it back to my family or even to charity. But, please, help her understand that this is my gift to her. I'm hoping we can live there together. But if not, I'd like to think that she, at least, will get to enjoy it.

I'd put off calling the attorney as long as I could. I just needed to get it over with. To find out what it was so I could deal with it.

So I called. And had to leave a message.

Peter looked at me in the rearview mirror.

"Are you okay, Mr. Worthington?"

I'd given up on Peter calling me by my first name. He insisted that according to the code of chauffeuring, he was bound to address me properly. I knew he was making it up, but it seemed to make him happy.

"Long day," I said.

"Let me know if you need anything," Peter said. "Happy to help."

"I know. Thank you."

The traffic finally started to clear and we were making progress toward my condo when the attorney returned my call.

He asked me to come in to his office in the morning. "I don't like to do these things over the phone."

"What kind of things are we talking about? All I have is this letter from Brady asking me to call you."

"Yes sir. That's how it works." I pulled the phone away from my ear and scowled at it. What was it with the formality today? Was I suddenly showing gray hair?

"Can you at least give me an idea? I'd like to be prepared."

The attorney hesitated. "I can't tell you because I haven't told Miss Grace yet."

"When is she coming in to see you?"

"In the morning."

"Good. I'll come with her."

"I don't know—"

"We'll see you in the morning," I said and hung up.

I didn't like people playing games like this. I just needed to take of whatever it was that Brady had been trying to do for Grace.

I could take care of her. He should have known I would.

Staring out the tinted window at the traffic flowing all

around us, it occurred to me that that could possibly be the problem.

I'd never told Brady how I felt about Grace. Not even once. Never even a hint.

But maybe on some level he knew.

Maybe he had somehow gotten the idea that I loved her and he wanted to take care of Grace himself.

He didn't want her having to rely on me.

Well, I decided. Whatever it was I would do whatever I could to make it happen.

It was Brady's last wish.

The least I could do was to honor it.

36

GRACE

*T*he next evening I stood in my new cozy bedroom in the Worthington's house and took my time changing clothes. I stepped out of my heels and set them in what was now my closet.

The first thing in my new closet.

It had been a big day.

I had accepted the job from Mrs. Savannah Worthington. She had been pleased, but had not seemed surprised.

She'd taken some time to give me a brief overview of some of the things I would be doing for her.

Then she'd had Peter drive me to the shelter to get my things. That part had been anticlimactic.

Mother Abigail had been meeting with a new girl. From the mere glimpse I'd caught of her, I knew this new girl was coming from an abusive home. I'd lived in the shelter long enough to know at a glance. There were also the dark glasses and the almost hidden bruise on her chin.

Maybe I should go into psychology like Savannah. I was good with people and I was intuitive. Surely those things would help me. With the right training, maybe I could be like Savannah, especially working for her.

I liked the idea. A lot.

At any rate, I'd had about two minutes to explain to Mother Abigail that I had found work and lodgings. She gave me a quick hug and wished me well.

My eyes actually stung a bit as I'd walked back down the stairs at the shelter for the last time.

Before, when I'd been leaving with Brady, I had been so intent on getting away, that it hadn't affect me like this.

Now that I'd been away, I knew in my heart that I wasn't coming back. I'd known the shelter was a quick stopover this time when I showed up a week ago.

I was a different person now with different circumstances.

And for some reason, it saddened me a bit. Another closed chapter in my life. Everything that had been familiar was now in the past.

I hadn't heard from Conner all day. Not since he'd left me here last night. It had been a little strange, staying behind at his grandparents' house while he drove off.

And I hadn't been able to fight the warm fuzzy feeling that had come over me as Savannah handed me a t-shirt and travel bag of toiletries.

It wasn't even odd that she had such things. She said one or another of her grandchildren often slept over without planning. It was no big deal.

So I tried not to let it be a big deal for me either.

Taking my book, I sat on the bed and checked my phone. It seemed to be working.

Allie came in, as though she sensed it was time for some sleep, and rubbed against me.

"What do you think, Allie?" I asked.

She purred in response.

"I think you're right. I think I'll talk to him tomorrow."

Curling up with the cat next to me, I soon lost myself in the book I was reading.

Tomorrow. Tomorrow I had to meet the attorney, then come back here to work. I'd see Conner Worthington soon enough. Right now I didn't have time to fret about him.

At least that's what I told myself.

37

CONNER

*I*t could probably be considered a little underhanded, but a guy had to use the resources at his disposal.

I asked my grandmother to keep Grace there so I could drive her to the attorney's office.

It probably would have been just as easy to call Grace, but for some reason I wanted it to be a surprise. Maybe I had a feeling she would want to her appointment with the attorney on her own.

Whatever it was, I showed up plenty early and found Grace and Grandma in Grandma's office.

Grandma was showing Grace her filing system.

They looked good together, I decided. The matriarch of the Worthington family and the girl who had my heart. The young and the old.

Grace's eyes lit up when she saw me.

"That's enough for now," Grandma said. "Conner's here, so he can drive you to your appointment."

"That's not necessary," Grace said.

"Take advantage of it while you can," Grandma said. "These pilots, they've always got somewhere to be."

"She's right," I said. "Let me drive you."

I still hadn't told anyone that I had a meeting with the attorney, too. It just didn't seem so important. The important thing was to get Grace there and get this whole thing over with.

Afterwards, I'd take her to lunch before I headed out to make my afternoon flight.

Grandma was right about that much. Pilots always had somewhere to be.

But right now that somewhere for me to be was with Grace.

In that moment, I saw the future stretch out before me.

I saw that I had two important things in my life. Flying and Grace. Not necessarily in that order.

But that wasn't how it was going to go. Brady had a last wish and it involved something he had done to provide for her. I had to push my images of the future aside.

As Grace darted upstairs to get her purse, Grandma sat back in her chair and locked her steely green gaze on mine.

"Be careful with this one," she said.

"You don't have to worry, Grandma." I sat down in the chair across from her.

"I know," she said. "You're a good man Conner Worthington."

"I realize she's still grieving," I said.

"Remember," she said. "Everyone grieves in their own way."

"What are you trying to tell me?"

"Not a thing," Grandma said.

Grace came back to the door before I had the chance to figure out what exactly Grandma was trying to tell me.

"You don't have to drive me," Grace said as we headed out the front door.

"You have other transportation lined up?"

"I do not," she said, sending me a look.

I grinned at her as I opened the passenger door and held out a hand to help her inside.

"Today I get to be your knight in shining armor."

"Ha. Then I guess I have no choice."

"Not even a little bit," I said before I closed her door.

As I walked around to the driver's side, I whistled that silly little happy tune again. I didn't even know what it was.

I liked being with her. I liked her.

And it didn't matter what we were doing.

It probably should.

It probably should matter that we were on the way to see an attorney about her dead fiancé.

Maybe I was messed up.

Maybe I would think about that later.

I climbed into the driver's seat and fastened my seatbelt.

Once we got all this business out of the way, I could take Grace on a flight.

She would like that.

I would like that.

Things were going to work out the way they were supposed to. That's what my grandmother always said. And Grandma Savannah was very wise. Very wise indeed.

We would see what this thing Brady had done was, then we would go from there.

It was all we could do.

38

GRACE

Although I'd felt at home in the Worthington's home, I felt intimidated at the attorney's office. So much so that I was thankful that Conner was with me.

It started with the receptionist. A beautiful young woman—in an icy kind of way—who, I swear, looked down her nose at me as she looked up from her seat behind the oversized counter. She scanned my identification. Conner's, too, though I didn't see why. After scanning mine, she slid it back with one finger as though she didn't want to touch it.

The counter was big enough to seat a family of twelve, yet hers seemed to be the only station.

Then there was the waiting room. Big enough to be someone's home. Perfect wood floors and two white leather sofas. The only other piece of furniture was a round table in the middle of the room with an oversized vase of white tulips. The whole room smelled clean, almost sterile, but a hint of vanilla.

Except for a siren in the far away distance, it was completely quiet in the space. No music. No phones ringing. No people talking.

All this on the twelfth floor of a skyscraper in the middle of downtown Houston.

I sat on the edge of my seat, Conner sitting next to me.

"Is this normal?" I asked.

"I guess so," he said. "I don't really know."

I nodded. And how would he know? This wasn't something everyone would experience. No one I had ever known had an attorney at a place like this. They would have no need to.

I had worked in a diner, for God's sake. No one who came in there and certainly no one who worked there had enough money to even take a breath in a place like this.

We'd been five minutes early and at eleven o'clock on the dot, the snotty receptionist called me back.

I stood up, feeling a little wobbly on my heels, and looked over my shoulder at Conner.

"Come with me," I said, trying to sound strong, but probably failing terribly at it. "Please."

"Of course." He was already getting to his feet.

The receptionist looked at Conner with an expression bordering between blank and just enough of a hint of flirtation that I saw it.

If Conner noticed, he showed no sign of it.

"Are you okay?" he asked as we walked down the wide hallway to the attorney's office.

I nodded. I would not have been okay if he hadn't been with me.

The receptionist deposited us in another, small waiting room. This one was of normal size, with only one white leather sofa.

"Why would Brady use an attorney here?" I asked, keeping my voice to a whisper.

"Probably something to do with his grandfather," he said. "I think his grandfather was an attorney."

"I didn't know that."

"Not many people did. Did you know that he was an only child?"

"I thought he had a sister."

"Stepsister."

That could mean a lot of things. But what I didn't understand was what it had to do with me. Brady and I hadn't married. I had no right to anything that belonged to him or his family. Didn't want or expect anything.

I wanted to move forward. To make my own way in the world.

Unless… unless they wanted to make sure I wasn't carrying his child. A child could complicate things.

But it was easy. I wasn't.

There was no need for all this formality.

I reached over and put a hand over Conner's.

I was thankful Conner was here with me, but I didn't want to be here.

39

CONNER

The attorney's office was unnecessarily pretentious. It was obviously meant to intimidate. And it did just that to Grace.

Now I was definitely glad I had come with her. She needed me. And I needed to get her out of here as soon as I could.

"It'll be fine," I said, probably to assure both of us.

I truly could not imagine Grace here by herself. She could handle herself, sure, but the intimidation factor was over the top.

I still hadn't told her that I, too, had been summoned here. I didn't think it was necessary and I didn't need to compound it this whole experience.

The attorney, finally, called us in.

At least the attorney, though not affable by any means, seemed to be somewhat approachable. I would even venture to say that he didn't seem to belong here in this building, but that was a tentative observation that I reserved the right to change.

We sat in three comfortable leather chairs in front of the floor to ceiling window with an incredible view of west Houston.

The attorney, wearing a white shirt, not jacket, but a tie tight at his neck, held a legal pad and a pen, but hadn't produced any papers. Perhaps he had everything memorized. With the money he charged, he probably should take the time to memorize his clients' information.

"Can I get you something to drink?"

"No," I said. "I'm good. Grace?"

"No thank you," she said. her spine was stiff and she sat on the edge of her chair. Now that we were in the attorney's office, she was hiding her nerves quite well.

Grace was not afraid to be vulnerable, but she was strong, too. I liked that about her.

I liked everything about her.

The attorney set his legal pad aside and leaned forward. After a quick glance at me, he locked his gaze on Grace.

"I have a feeling Brady didn't tell you everything," he said.

Grace glanced at me. "I'm sure you're right."

I'd already told her things she hadn't known, even while we had been sitting in the attorney's private waiting room.

Having known Brady since we were boys, I knew things that his family had managed to bury for the most part over the years.

Things about his grandfather that the family had moved past a long time ago.

Apparently Brady had been dealing with it, though, enough to have an attorney on hand to put everything together for him.

"Brady had some money," he said. "From his grandfather."

Grace kept her expression blank, her gaze steady on the attorney.

"He invested in something he told me he thought you would like. But to do so, he had to sell his grandfather's property."

Grace glanced at me now.

"What kind of property?" she asked.

"The details aren't relevant at this point," Attorney Whitehouse said. "But they do speak to the level of deep affection that Brady held for you. And they also speak to the gravity of the decision he made."

I had an inkling what the attorney was talking about. Brady's grandfather had owned a ranch in south Houston. I'd been there a couple of times. Thousands of acres and a small mansion sitting in the middle of it. Surely not…

"The ranch?" I asked.

"Yes," Attorney Whitehouse said. "He found a buyer with no trouble, considering this market."

"So he sold his property," Grace said, getting us back on track. I heard the impatience in her voice, one that echoed my own.

Whitehouse turned his attention back to Grace and he actually gave her what could almost resemble a smile.

"He told me you have a fondness for Japan."

"Japan." Grace sat back, her eyes wide. "I don't— We lived there for a time. We were going to…"

"You're studying the language."

"I was. Some. I try to make the best of any situation I find myself in."

Whitehouse picked up his legal pad, scribbled something that was nothing.

"You have no family. Is that correct?"

Grace glanced at me, obviously uncomfortable.

"What is this about?" I asked, taking her hand.

Whitehouse narrowed his eyes and his gaze flicked to our hands for a split second. "I'm just checking some facts. No need to be alarmed."

"I'm not alarmed," I said. But I was concerned. I still didn't know where this was headed.

Whitehouse set his legal pad down again and leaned forward, his hands clasped.

"Grace," he said. "Brady bought a villa and listed you as the beneficiary."

"A villa?" She did look somewhat alarmed now. And something else. A little pale. She shook her head. "What kind of villa?"

"A house." Whitehouse looked at me, narrowing his eyes. "His last wish is that Grace live in that villa."

"Okay," I said, feeling Grace bristle next to me. "Where is the villa?"

"The villa is off the coast of Japan."

40

GRACE

"I need some air," I said, springing out of my seat and rushing toward the heavy, oversized door. My heels clicked on the wood floors. Wood floors that were used to far more expensive shoes than the ones on my feet that I had bought at the outlets mall.

I rushed down the hall, past the snotty receptionist, out the glass door to the hallway, to the elevator.

I pressed the button. Even though it lit up, I pressed it twice more.

My vision was cloudy and I was having trouble seeing.

Someone came up behind me. I hoped it was Conner. Heaven help anyone else who tried to approach me right now.

"Grace," Conner said.

The elevator opened and I got on, Conner at my heels.

"I need some air," I said again. I felt like I'd been suffocating in the stuffy, overly elegant offices.

Since I just stood there, not pressing a button, Conner did. Conner pressed the button for the lobby and the elevator began to move.

I looked over at Conner. I didn't try to hide the pain. I couldn't have if I'd wanted to.

"Why did he do that?" I asked.

Conner just shook his head.

"He loved you," he said.

Pressing my fingertips against my forehead, I closed my eyes.

"He sold his ranch."

"You knew about the ranch?"

"No," I said. "But it was a ranch. Here. In Texas."

The elevator doors opened and we stepped off.

I didn't know which way to go. I was all turned around. So I just stood there.

The security guard, sitting behind a counter, with his arms crossed, watched us closely.

"Come with me," Conner said, taking my hand.

He led me through a glass door to a little garden on the inside of the building.

We sat on a concrete bench, surrounded by trees and flowers, butterflies lighting here and there. Somewhere in the back of my mind, I was struck by the incongruence of the attorney's office we had just left and this inviting courtyard garden.

I clasped my hands together in my lap to keep them from trembling.

I couldn't think. Didn't know what to think even if I could.

But Conner was here. Conner would help me sort this out.

"A villa?" I asked, searching Conner's gaze.

I knew perfectly well what a villa was. That wasn't my question at all, despite the way the attorney had seemed to think I needed an explanation.

"You told me you liked Japan," he said. "That you were learning the language."

"Of course I was," I said. "We lived there."

"Brady really loved you to do that," Conner said.

Didn't he know that was the wrong thing to say?

I already knew that he loved me. I knew it and I didn't want to be reminded just how much.

"What am I going to do with a villa in Japan?" I asked, keeping my gaze straight ahead, watching two butterflies land briefly on a pink daisy before flying off again.

Conner looked at me for a few moments, not saying anything.

"There's only one thing to do," he said.

"What? What am I supposed to do?"

"You have to live there."

41

CONNER

rady had brought me into this and now I had to do my part.

Grace and I sat on a concrete bench in the courtyard far below the stuffy attorney's building. The cold concrete was a reminder not to get too comfortable here. This was a place of serious business. I didn't get the purpose of the flowers. Probably a tax write-off.

There was a slight breeze coming over the one side of the building that was single story. The other three sides were various levels.

It was an interesting design that I wouldn't mind seeing more of. But not right now.

Right now I had to help Grace navigate this unexpected thing that had fallen into her lap.

Brady had taken his family's legacy, essentially cashed it in, and invested in a foreign home. A villa.

What the hell had he been thinking?

He wanted Grace to live in Japan? Alone?

"What do I do?" Grace asked, looking at me now.

I thought about Brady. About our lifelong friendship. He

and I had been closer than brothers. We had always put our friendship first. Women would come and go, but we remained steadfast. That was why I had deferred my feelings for Grace to him. Conflict over her would have destroyed our friendship.

And now he had asked me for one final thing. One final request. As much as it hurt my heart, I had to do it.

"I think you have to give it a try," I said.

"A try?" She was scowling at me now. I did my best to ignore it.

"Yes. Brady loved you and he bought this villa for the two of you."

Grace's eyes were glazed with unshed tears and she was looking to me for guidance.

My heart wanted me to tell her that she didn't have to go. That she should stay here.

"At least find out more about it," I said. "Get more information. Then you can decide what to do."

She lifted her chin and turned away.

I couldn't begin to imagine what she must be thinking.

I wanted to pull her to me. To hold her and comfort her. To tell her she didn't have to do anything she didn't want to.

But Brady's last wish for me was to get Grace to the villa he had bought for them. And if not for them, then for her.

The world was a global place. And as the attorney so insensitively pointed out, Grace had no family here. No ties to hold her back.

She could go.

That's what she should do. And I could not be the one to hold her back.

"So you think I should go. To live in Japan."

"It's not about what I want," I said. It hurt me, but I steeled myself. I could so easily sway her. I could sway her to stay here.

But that would not be right. This was supposed to be her decision.

One she had to make.

I had been wrong to befriend her so quickly after Brady's death. Now I could see why people advised against such things. There was unfinished business between a couple, married or not, that others couldn't possibly know about after one passed away suddenly. This was a perfect illustration of that.

"Grace," I said, looking into her eyes. "This is something you have to do for yourself. It's not for me to decide or even to state my opinion."

The words hurt me as much as they hurt her. But the tears filling her eyes hurt me worse than they hurt her.

This was the hardest thing I had ever had to do.

I tried to swallow past the lump in my throat, but it just made the back of my throat burn.

"Come on," I said, standing up, keeping my hands to myself. "Let's go up and get all the paperwork done while we're here. So we don't have to come back to this place."

42

———

GRACE

*I*t was all said and done now, as they said.

Alone now, I sat on the bed in my bedroom in the Worthingtons' house and stared at the papers strewn over the bed.

I had managed to make it from Conner's car to my bedroom without having to talk to or even see anyone else. I counted myself fortunate in that matter.

It was about the only thing I counted myself fortunate about right about now.

Nothing else was as it should be.

Everything had been going so well.

I'd gotten out of the shelter. I'd known I wouldn't be there long, but it was still good to have secured a job, especially one that came with room and board.

My eyes brimming with tears, I looked out the window at the magnolia trees, branches swaying, their blooms fluttering in the wind.

There was a storm brewing.

Usually, I had an interest in all things weather, but not today.

Today I had no interest in much of anything other than... this.

Truthfully, I wanted all this to go away.

I lay back crossways on the bed and stared at the ceiling.

Something had flipped with Conner. He had been affectionate until the visit with the attorney, but...

Even though it was the last thing I wanted to think about, I replayed the events of the meeting. The whole nightmare of it.

I'd had to sign a million papers. Accepted a house... a villa... I didn't even want. Had I had a choice? I hadn't seemed like it at the time.

And Conner had signed something.

My thoughts stopped.

And I sat up, my feet sliding easily to the floor.

I'd thought he was signing as a witness to my signature, but he'd had his own paper to sign.

Why?

I looked through the copies strewn on the bed. Papers that made me sick just to look at.

My God. Why would Brady buy a villa in Japan without at least telling me, much less asking me about it?

I didn't have a copy of anything Conner had signed.

Then... What?

Maybe just that he had attended the meeting. An office as stuffy as the, what was his name, Whitehouse office, probably had paperwork for going to the bathroom.

I got up and went to stare out the window at the lightning flashing in the distance.

This storm could delay some flights.

Leaning against the window ledge, I shook my head. Conner had me thinking about things like flights.

He'd been going to take me on a flight.

Maybe even Mackinac Island. He hadn't actually said it, but he'd made me believe that it was possible.

I turned and looked at the bed.

All my dreams had evaporated beneath the weight of that villa. In Japan.

I hadn't complained about going to Japan with Brady. It was part of his job in the military.

But me? I was an all-American girl and I didn't mind who knew it or what they thought about it. I bled red, white, and blue.

I did not want to go to Japan. I'd just gotten back from there. I certainly did NOT want to live in Japan. Or own a home in Japan.

But it looked like I had no choice.

Brady had made my choices for me.

"Why?" I asked out loud. "Why did you do this to me?"

43

—————

CONNER

It was one of those stormy summer days, winds and dangerous dark clouds racing sideways across the state of Texas.

The storm brewed and gathered as it approached the eastern side of the state.

Later that afternoon I had to fly to Dallas to pick Steve up and bring him back to Houston.

To say that I was in a foul mood, would be an understatement.

I'd gotten out of Houston before the storm, but would probably catch it on the other end and get stuck in Dallas tonight.

At this point I didn't care.

I'd done the honorable thing with Grace.

I'd been a perfect gentleman and a good friend. Even if the two things didn't exactly line up together at this point.

I taxied along the runway until I reached the private terminal area. Skye Travels had a small terminal here. One that we actually used frequently.

It was a necessary convenience, as so many of our

customers flew between the two Texas cities of Houston and Dallas. Besides that, it was a little known fact that Grandpa Noah had actually started Skye Travels in Dallas—before he and Grandma Savannah decided to move to Houston.

I went through my checklists, made sure Steve had plenty of cold water to drink. It was really the only thing he ever asked for.

With everything ready for the flight back to Houston, I left the plane and went into the terminal to grab a hot coffee before the flight back.

It made no sense, but all I wanted to do was to get back to Houston. To my condo. Maybe have a beer and stare out over the city.

I wasn't good company right now.

That was one thing I was certain about.

Being a perfect gentleman and good friend had cost me happiness.

Taking my cup of hot coffee, I went back outside to wait for Steve. The clouds coming in from the west brought slightly tolerably not so hot weather. I wouldn't go so far as to describe it as cool weather.

According to the radar, this was a different band of storms from the one that was over Houston right now.

It wouldn't hurt if we went ahead and left. If we left now, we could get out of here ahead of this storm and land in Houston after that one had moved out.

I looked at my watch again. Steve was late.

I checked my phone for messages. Anytime he'd ever been late, he had sent me a text or called.

No messages from Steve.

Having my fill of the mugginess, I went back inside, into the air conditioning to wait.

I paced the terminal.

I was a little worried about Steve, but my thoughts were consumed with thoughts of Grace.

Pacing the terminal floor, I stewed about her.

I could have swayed her so easily. I don't think she even wanted to go to Japan.

But she was grieving.

And grief was something she had to deal with. In her own way.

My way of dealing with it was to be supportive of her and Brady's wishes for her at the same time.

"Mr. Worthington," the receptionist asked as I paced near her desk. "Have you heard from Steve?"

"No," I said, checking my phone again. He was an hour late.

"I'll call him," I said, tapping his number and turning away.

The phone rang three times and went to voicemail. I hung up. Ran a hand through my hair. Something wasn't right.

I turned around in a complete circle. Then dialed his number again.

"Hello." A young man answered the phone. I ran through what I knew about Steve. Did he have family in Dallas? Not that I knew of.

"I'm calling for Steve."

"Steve is at Dallas General Hospital. Do you know if he has any family?"

44

GRACE

I barely slept, but by the time I woke the next morning, I had made my decision.

I would just go.

I would go to Japan and see what was up with the villa. I wasn't making any guarantees that I would live there permanently, but I needed to go. To see it.

It was something I had to do. Besides, the cards seem to have fallen where they would.

So I showered and packed all my things. And still had room left in my suitcase.

It broke my heart when I took my high heels out of the now empty closet.

I had been so very excited about this job. About working for Savannah

Worthington. About living here.

About Conner.

But Conner had turned cold.

If a man could turn that cold that easily, it meant he didn't want anything serious.

He'd been fine with casual friendship. Holding hands even.

But if I'd made the decision to stay here because of him, he would have felt obligated to me and he obviously didn't want that.

So I had to save us both the embarrassment of expecting anything more from each other and just go.

After making a quick run through the house, I learned that the Worthingtons had taken an unplanned flight up to Dallas.

I was pretty sure Conner had flown to Dallas yesterday after he'd dropped me off here. After the disaster that was the meeting with the attorney.

But that wasn't my business. Conner was no longer my business… if he ever was.

The butler offered a call a car to take me to the airport, so I accepted.

Thirty minutes later, I went outside, and walked down the damp sidewalk to the car. The driver, Peter, followed with my suitcase.

After I was settled into the backseat of the car, Peter turned around and looked at me.

"The airport?" he asked. "Did I understand that correctly?"

"Yes," I said, straightening in my seat. I could do this. I gave him my gate terminal.

He shoved his shades back over his eyes and turned around, not making any comment.

My heart broke as he drove along the circle drive and turned onto Memorial Drive headed toward the freeway.

We were on our way to the airport.

I was on my way to Japan.

Sitting quietly I watched as we drove past the old established houses, some old, some new. All big. Mostly hidden behind thick brick fences.

A section of sidewalk was blocked off and a construction crew was replacing the concrete. Progress. Always progress.

My eyes felt heavy. Houston had my heart as much as any

city could. I'd left here once on an adventure that had turned out not to be so much a good adventure and now I didn't care to leave again.

We'd no more than gotten on the freeway, when Peter slowed down.

Traffic.

Traffic was at a standstill.

"There's an accident up ahead," Peter told me over his shoulder.

There was an accident on the freeway and the wind was picking up.

Maybe. Just maybe I'd get lucky and my flight would be delayed.

Or not. It would be better, I decided, to just get the trip over with.

Maybe I'd stay in Japan for a while. Take some time to figure out what I wanted to do with the rest of my life.

It seems Brady had made sure I wouldn't be working in a diner anymore.

After reading the fine print in the documents, I'd discovered that staying in the villa came with a generous stipend from an account Brady had set up. I was unclear about whether the stipend was contingent upon living in the villa or not. I'd have to ask the attorney, but that conversation would have to wait. Maybe I would email him. Talking to Whitehouse was not something I cared to do.

After my thoughts settled, I used the time sitting in traffic to think about the one thing I probably shouldn't be thinking about.

Conner Worthington.

45

CONNER

Monitors beeped. Doors opened and closed. The clean scent was stifling.

I sat in what was supposed to pass for a comfortable armchair next to the hospital bed where Steve lay, hooked up to all sorts of monitors.

I'd come straight here when I'd learned he had had a heart attack.

I wasn't family, but the doctor knew my grandfather and they liked Steve. Since Steve had no family, I was allowed to sit with him.

And, I glanced at my watch, Grandma and Grandpa would be arriving here within the hour.

I hadn't known they were quite as close to Steve as all that, but there were lots of things I didn't know.

A pretty nurse came in, checked vitals and changed out bags of fluids.

"I brought you a heated blanket," she said. "It might be hot outside, but it's always cold in here."

"Thank you." I took the blanket, and laid it over the arm of the chair. I was enjoying the air conditioning, but I didn't tell her.

After the nurse left, I leaned back, dozed off, after I grew tired of watching the steady monitors.

"Surely you have something better to do than sit with an old man," Steve said, his voice raspy.

"Steve." I sat up, wiping my face with my hands and leaning forward. "How do you feel? Do you need anything?"

"One of the nurses will be here in a few seconds to give me some ice in a cup."

I grinned.

"You see," he said as another nurse, this one not so friendly did just as he predicted. Just as the other nurse had done not thirty minutes earlier she took his blood pressure. Checked the monitors.

"What happened?" I asked.

"The old ticker needed some work," he said.

"They said you had a heart attack."

"Maybe," he said. "Probably some plague buildup. They cleared it all out."

"You don't seem too worried," I said. I'd been in the hospital for less than three hours and I felt more drained than he looked.

"I'll be okay," he said.

"I hope so," I said, mostly to myself. His lack of concern was not what I expected.

"So, how is it going?" he asked. "With Grace?"

Had I told him about Grace? Sometimes I talked too much.

"Nothing. Nothing is going to happen."

Steve, in a very non-Steve like way just looked at me, not saying anything.

"Brady gave her a villa." I blurted.

"A what? A house?"

"Yeah," I said. "In Japan."

Steve took a bite of ice and looked at me like I'd started speaking a foreign language. Like maybe I was the one who needed to be in the hospital bed.

"I think you need to run that one by me again," he said. "They're giving me so much medicine. I think I must have heard you wrong."

I rather felt the same way. Like surely I had heard something wrong. Like I'd missed a step somewhere and lost my footing. It happened.

46

GRACE

By the time we reached the airport and neared the drop off area, the rain was coming down in sheets. Sideways.

I'd gotten a text from the airline. My flight was delayed until further notice. No planes were taking off in this weather. Not small planes and not large planes.

"How long is your flight delayed?" Peter asked as we sat in traffic again.

"It just says cancelled."

"I'll drive you home," he said. "You can reschedule."

Home.

He wanted to take me home.

But I didn't know where home was right now.

While we'd been sitting in traffic, I'd had plenty of time to tie up some loose ends.

I'd texted Savannah. Thanked her profusely and apologized for changing my mind about the job. It made me sick to my stomach to send it even if I had explained that I had to go to Japan. Conner would explain it all to her. She would understand. She had to.

She hadn't responded. Probably still in flight to Dallas. Or maybe she wouldn't bother.

I'd already closed the door at the shelter. So that wasn't home.

The attorney had given me a debit card. One that apparently was linked to an account that was at my disposal.

I didn't want it. But I had not been in a position to refuse it either.

It probably would not have been so bad if I didn't have so much guilt.

Brady had loved me. Had taken care of me.

And all I could think about was his best friend. Conner.

About how I didn't want to go to Japan. I wanted to stay here.

With Conner.

To be part of his family.

"It's okay," I said "I'll just wait in the airport."

"You can't wait in the airport," Peter said. "You don't know how long it'll be."

I knew that. But I needed to do it.

I needed some distance between me and the Worthingtons.

Some time to get my head straight.

If he took me back there, it would just make it that much harder for me to leave.

"Really," I said. "I want to wait here. I *need* to wait here."

I could see his eyes narrowed as he looked at me in the mirror. If he'd just think about it, he would put it all together. I was here. Leaving the country. Conner was not here.

It had to be obvious.

"Okay," he said. "But if you change your mind at any time for any reason, you have to call me. I'll come right back."

"You're very kind," I said. "Too kind."

He pulled under the covered unloading area and went around to open my door.

Holding out a hand, he helped me out me out of the car. Had this been what Conner was doing? Just being kind like he would to anyone else?

"Miss Grace," he said. "I don't know what's happening, but promise me you'll let me know if you want me to come get you. I'll drive you anywhere you want to go. And if you don't have anywhere to go, you can camp out with me and my wife until you figure something out.

We've got a decent couch."

"No. I could never intrude that way," I said, but in truth, I was overwhelmed by his kindness.

He left me standing there while he unloaded my suitcase.

"International flights can be tricky," he said as he rolled the suitcase in my direction. "Don't get stuck in this airport too long before you call me."

"Okay," I said with a smile, then turned away and used every last ounce of strength I had left to walk away from the one last familiar thing in my world.

I walked through the doors and joined the ranks of people going somewhere not here.

47

CONNER

y the time I landed at the Houston airport, the passing storm was no more than a distant memory. Any lingering moisture dried up from the hellacious heat.

Steve and I had a conversation about Grace that lasted about five minutes before I realized that I was an idiot.

I'd already been pretty sure I was an idiot, but he just clarified it for me.

"There's nothing I can do at this point," I'd told him.

"You're right. You certainly can't do anything sitting here with an old man."

That was right about the time I got the message from Peter.

PETER: *Just dropped Grace off at international terminal. Flight delayed. Thought you might want to know.*

Damn right I wanted to know.

"She's on her way to Japan," I told Steve.

"Get out of here," Steve said, with an irritation I'd never heard him use. "I don't care where you go, just get out of here."

"I don't—"

"And I don't want to see you again until you have this

straightened out." He shooed me away with a wave of his hand and turned his head away from me.

He'd been right, of course. He had to be right.

It hadn't been hard for me to find out which flight Grace was supposed to be on.

If Peter's information was correct, then Grace was still at the airport.

She probably didn't know it, but she could be there for days before she could get on another flight. Nothing was like it used to be.

It was okay though. Gave me enough time to find her.

It was my fault she was going anyway.

I'd taken Brady's request to heart. And I'd acted on it against my own judgement.

And he had merely been acting on the information he had at the time. Four months ago. He'd made his will four months ago. Just one month after they had gotten to Japan. Before he had known he would be going on a mission that would turn out to be deadly.

But Brady had been a good man. A man who prepared.

What didn't add up for me was why he hadn't married Grace already.

He'd done everything as though they were married. Put her in his will. Buying the villa.

But something was missing.

Whatever it was, I would never know.

But what I did know was that life was for the living.

And now that Brady was gone, it was my turn to take of care Grace. My turn to be with her.

And I wasn't going to let her slip through my fingers.

Not this time.

I'd let it happen one time.

Fate had brought her back to me and I couldn't help but think that meant something.

It meant something to me.

To me it was a responsibility and a gift all rolled into one.

So I would find her.

And see if she would have me.

If it was too soon for her, I would wait.

Just as Brady had waited, I would wait.

Brady had waited too long.

But I wasn't going to wait too long.

48

GRACE

In a chair against the glass wall, I stayed out of the way.

My flight had been rescheduled for seven p.m. Not nearly as long a wait as Peter had me expecting.

So many people coming and going. I'd flown a few times now, but I hadn't actually spent much time in airports. Not like this. And certainly not in an international terminal.

I put the people around me into three categories. The businessmen. Obviously. Vacationers. Those were easy to spot, too. Either families with bored and impatient kids fidgeting or crying Two people sitting close. Talking quietly. Holding hands.

Then there was the anomaly. Like me. Someone without an obvious purpose for flying to Tokyo.

There was the grandmother sitting alone. Passing the time with her knitting while she waited for her flight. Probably on her way to visit a family member. Maybe a son or daughter who had moved out of the country.

There was the teenage boy with the backpack. Looked

almost too young for college. But maybe a foreign exchange student. Maybe high schools were doing exchanges now.

It didn't take me long before I got tired of trying to figure out why people were traveling to Japan.

My brain kept wandering back to Conner. I would have stayed. But he seemed like he wanted me to go. If I stayed here, maybe he felt responsible for me.

I set the Starbuck's cold brew coffee I'd lost my taste for on the floor and checked the time on my phone again.

Two hours before we should start boarding.

I distracted myself by typing in the address of the villa. Again.

It was a simple house on the coast. Staged. I didn't know if the furniture was still there or if I was going to have to furnish it.

It was still hard to wrap my head around why Brady had sold his family legacy to buy a villa in a foreign country. He'd bought the villa outright, then put the remainder of the money in the bank.

Needing to pass the time, I opened the electronic file of documents the attorney had emailed me a couple of hours ago and started to read.

It didn't take long for me to learn something the attorney hadn't told me.

The sale of the ranch and subsequent purchase of the villa had been activated upon his death.

I looked up and gazed unseeingly toward the traffic passing along the hallway. A car packed with people passed, moving at a snail's pace. It looked out of place in this airport world where everyone was in a hurry.

Upon his death. How had Brady done that? Did that mean he had not *really* intended for all this to happen? If he had lived, would he had have gone back to the attorney and changed his will?

Taking a deep breath, I dove back into the paperwork. It not only passed the time, but I was curious now.

It was an hour later when I looked up again, my eyes weary from reading the small print on my phone.

I blamed the attorney for not giving me these papers while I was at his office, but he was an ass. He probably did it on purpose.

I stretched, looked up, and squinted.

Another cluster of airline staff hurried past. Pretty people. They were pretty people in their own world. Passengers were just customers. They paid us no mind.

Another pilot, this one walking by himself approached more slowly. He caught my attention because he was walking slower than everyone else.

Then he turned and looked right at me.

Something deep in my gut clenched.

My composure shattered like a glass ball dropping against a concrete sidewalk.

Conner Worthington was walking right toward me.

49

CONNER

There were definite benefits to being Noah Worthington's grandson. That and my card identifying me as a pilot had gotten me past security into the passenger's only area of the airport.

I knew the airport well enough. Well enough to find Grace without any problem. I'd never aspired to work as a commercial pilot. I didn't see the point of it when I had my family's company to play in. And I didn't mind telling people I worked for my family. My grandfather didn't hire just anyone. Only the best. And that meant family was not an automatic shoe in. We had to earn our way just like everybody else.

Grace sat with her back to the window, the evening sun, poised to begin its downward decent into darkness, glowing around her.

She had her hair pulled back and as I neared her, I saw the sadness was back in her eyes.

That sadness hadn't been there the last few days. The last few days, she'd looked happy.

I'd did that, I realized with load of regret falling over my head.

Thank God for thunderstorms and flight delays.

If not for uncontrollable events, she'd be on her way to Japan right now.

I had to give it to her. The girl made decisions fast and acted faster.

When we'd been sitting in the attorney's office, I hadn't known if she was going to Japan at all, much less right away.

I sat down in the seat next to her.

"Headed somewhere?" I asked, sweeping a lock of hair that had fallen loose out of the clip that held her hair back.

"I was," she said, licking her red, lipstick free lips. "But… the storm…"

"It was a bad one. Bad in Dallas, too."

"How are you here?"

"I have connections," I said with a grin. And an uncanny sense of dodging storms when I needed to.

"Okay," she said. "*Why* are you here?"

"Sometimes, like most men, I do things for what seems like the right reason, but it's actually the wrong reason."

She just looked blankly at me.

I took a deep breath and started again, this time jumping into the deep end.

"Don't go," I said, taking her hands. "Don't go to Japan. I know it's probably weird for you. Me being Brady's best friend and all. You being engaged to him. And it's so soon. But ever since that night two years ago when I first saw you I knew. I knew you were the one for me. But then Brady—"

She put her arms around me, stopping my rambling.

I gathered her up in my arms and sat back down with her in my lap. Pressed my forehead against hers.

"I knew it, too," she said.

And then her lips pressed against mine and everything slid into place.

Grace was my girl now.

EPILOGUE
GRACE

"There's a fort," I said, not taking my eyes off the ground below.

"I know," Conner said, his voice coming through my headphones loud and clear.

"Make another pass," I said with a glance over my shoulder at him.

He laughed and turned the wheel to start another pass around Mackinac Island.

I looked down at the Grand Hotel with the longest porch in the world. Even from here I could see the horse and carriages below. No cars.

Then I saw the houses along the coast of Lake Huron. As beautiful as any beach. The fishing piers. A church steeple. The old iron cannons pointing out over the lake.

"Do we have time to take a tour of the fort?" I asked, already knowing the answer.

I could ask Conner to fly me to the moon and he'd turn over every rock trying to find a way to make it happen.

"We can do anything you want to do," he said.

I smiled. As we turned into the sun, the Tiffany diamond on my ring finger caught a glimmer of light.

Conner had moved quickly and I had gone right along with him.

We'd had no hesitation going forward. Instead we barreled forward into our life together.

If anyone questioned us and our rapid movement forward, no one said anything to us. On the contrary, everyone—everyone being Conner's family—had been so supportive.

Since I had no family, I had adopted his family.

And was happier than I had ever been. Ever.

"Ready to land?" he asked.

"Yes," I said, smiling over at him and sitting back in my seat. I checked my harness out of habit and watched as Conner went through the process of taking the plane down to the runway.

The landing was perfectly smooth as always.

I'd flown with Conner at least a dozen times now and he had perfect landings every time.

Removing my headphones, I looked around while Conner taxied back to the little building that served as a terminal.

A horse and carriage waited for us. Details. Conner was good with details.

He was so handsome just looking at him nearly took my breath away.

And when he looked at me with those sparkling blue eyes, like he was doing right now, my heart melted. Like it was doing right now.

I'd been under Conner Worthington's spell since the moment I'd first laid eyes on him.

If I'd ever doubted love at first sight being a real thing, I knew now just how real it was.

No more doubt.

And I was now a firm believer in fate.

Conner opened his door and cool air spilled inside the cockpit of the small Cessna.

Although it was late May, it was full on spring on Mackinac Island. And along with spring the air was still cool. Perfect even.

A complete turnaround from Houston where we had left just hours ago. It was amazing how different a few hours and a quick flight could make.

I unhooked my safety harness and waited for Conner to come around and open my door.

My nerves were buzzing with excitement. It was our first weekend away. And we were here at the island where the movie Somewhere in Time came to life.

He opened the door and put his strong hands on my waist as he helped me down.

Before setting me on the ground, he twirled me around. My hands clasped behind his neck, I was helpless to do anything other than grin.

My skirt belled out around me and I felt like a fairy princess as he slowly let me slide down until my feet touched the ground of Mackinac Island for the first time.

He caught my lips in a kiss. A kiss that held all the magic I felt every minute I was with him.

The twists and turns of my life had gotten me right here right now at this very perfect moment.

He pressed his forehead against mine.

"Are you ready for an adventure?" he asked.

"Everything with you is an adventure," I said.

"Our carriage awaits," he said as he took my hand and led me toward the horse and carriage waiting to take us to the Grand Hotel.

I loved the way my life had settled. I wouldn't change a single thing.

The snow globe that was my life was a beautiful, magical place to be.

Keep Reading for a preview of
WRITTEN IN THE WIND...

PREVIEW WRITTEN IN THE WIND

Sophia Becquerel

I stepped over a two-by-four, my work boots sending up a plume of sawdust. The buzz of the table saws mixed with steady pop of air powered nail guns to create a cacophony found only at construction sites.

Stopping at a door frame, I dropped my clipboard to my waist and studied the distance of the opening to the wall.

"Here's your helmet, Miss Becquerel," Frederick said, handing me a white hardhat.

"I don't need—" Frederick put his hands on his hips. "Never mind." I took the hat, though I honestly saw no point in it. No one was working overhead.

"Thank you." I put the hat on my head and smiled at Frederick. He was a middle-aged man—gray hair, obviously handsome in his younger years and still accustomed to using that to his advantage.

It wasn't fair to him that I was coming in now after he'd already gotten this far. Frederick was a good architect, one of the best in the state and THE best in Natchez.

And just because I had a degree from one of the best architecture schools in the country, didn't mean he didn't have more experience.

I'd seen the blueprints and I knew what he was trying to do.

I had no problem with him replicating a house built hundreds of years ago, but there were always things that could be done better. There was no reason not to take advantage of knowledge gleaned over those hundreds of years, especially since central air conditioning, running water, and electricity had to be taken into account. And not to forget a modern kitchen built inside the house, not in an outbuilding.

Besides, I couldn't help myself.

I put a hand on the door frame.

"I hate to ask this, but do you think you could move this door down about…" I held my tape measure to the floor. "four and a half feet?"

Frederick rubbed his chin and gave a valiant effort toward hiding his disappointment.

"Sure," he said, making a note on his own clipboard. "Not a problem."

"Thank you."

I stepped through what would be the doorway. This would be the study.

The tall French windows would look out over the Mississippi River. It was a good view. Better than Grandpa Jonathan's view.

"Quitting time," one of the men called.

"Who made you the boss?" Another man asked, but all the saws turned off and the sounds of construction turned to sounds of men tossing tools into their tool boxes.

"Nobody's gonna argue with the clock," a third man said and the men laughed.

"Looks like the men are quitting for the day," Frederick said. "I'll stay 'til you're ready to go."

"Not a chance." I turned and looked at him. "I can think better alone anyway."

"You sure?"

Frederick was probably trying to decide if letting me think was a good thing or not.

"Absolutely," I said. "When I'm finished, I'll walk over to Grandpa's house."

"Text me when you get there, will you? Your father would tear me to shreds if something happened to you."

"I will." I turned away, waiting for the men to leave so I could get focused again. I'd ridden out here with Frederick, so I could see his point.

It was a fifteen-minute walk back to Grandpa's. Five if I jogged it. I knew because I'd jogged it this morning before I drove into town to get a copy of the plat. Asking the clerk to send over an electronic copy had gotten me transferred to two different people before I'd politely been told that they didn't do that here.

As the men drove off, I removed the helmet and took a deep breath.

Now I could really get a sense of how the house was going to feel.

I was pretty sure there had been a garçonnière here at some point—many long years ago… certainly not in my lifetime.

It was in the perfect spot to catch the breeze coming off the river and it was just far enough away from what had been the main house—now my grandfather's house—to allow the older boys privacy. Living in their own apartment, but still on the property allowed boys to be on their own while still being part of the family and helping out with the crops.

I walked around a bit, checking the general layout. The house was just a skeleton at this point.

If I'd know about it soon enough, I would have been the lead architect myself. But that would have required me being closer than I was to my father and not just in physical proximity.

I hadn't planned on spending my first summer after college graduation in Mississippi. Top in my class at MIT, I'd had three job offers in the Boston area. I'd ultimately chosen the one that allowed me to start in September.

And all because of one phone call from my father.

He was retiring from the Air Force after a full twenty-year career and was building a house on his father's land.

The timing was a bit off though. Father's retirement wasn't until October, but he wanted the house to be move in ready when he got here. With his new wife.

My momma could not have cared less. She had married her college sweetheart when they'd accidentally reconnected on Facebook.

According to her, she'd searched for him after her divorce from my father, but hadn't been able to find him. Then through the magic of Facebook, he had gotten a spontaneous friend request. He had accepted, messaged her, and there had been no turning back for them. They lived in France now. I missed her, but I was proud of her for following her dream and not letting anything hold her back.

In that way she was my hero and my role model. I had no college sweetheart to reconnect with, but I had gone to Boston, an unfamiliar city, on my own.

Father and I had never been close. Always at work, the Air Force was his life. But to his credit, he'd always taken care of his four children, even after the divorce.

It was going to be dark soon. And despite my insistence that I could get to my grandfather's house safely, walking in the woods at night was not something I cared to do.

Still… I wanted to take some notes, so I sat on a bench, in what would be the parlor, the guys had thrown together for themselves and turned to a blank page.

At first the music was faint... barely noticeable. Then it slowly got louder, until I couldn't help but notice it.

It was classical music... piano.

It was too loud to be coming from Grandpa's house.

When I looked up, the bright setting sun was in my eyes.

My vision still blinded by the sun, I put a hand over my eyes and looked to my right.

I saw people... men... and ladies... Waltzing. The ladies were wearing long hoop-skirted dresses that swayed as they twirled.

A vase of fresh white roses was in a vase at my right hand, where a side table would be.

There were three couples dancing and one man standing off by himself, a glass in hand.

I closed my eyes, squeezing them tightly together. Oddly enough, it seemed to help the music fade slowly into the background.

But when I opened my eyes, the dancers were still there.

The room was fully furnished, much as I imagined it being completed. A fire burning gently in the fireplace. Tall windows framed with emerald green curtains. The furniture was pushed back against the walls.

The one man, dressed in what looked like a black tux with a white cravat, leaning with one elbow on the mantle, seemed to look right at me.

His handsome face wore a confident expression. I couldn't tell if he was looking at me or through me.

I pressed my fingers against my brow and closed my eyes again.

I was imagining things. I'd gotten swept away in visualizing the completed house.

Shaking my head, I slowly opened one eye, then the other.

The sun had dropped below the horizon now and again I was surrounded by the barely framed skeleton of the house.

I blew out a breath and stood up. My knees were weak, so I sat back down to give myself a minute.

It was going to be dark soon.

I needed to pull myself together and get to my grandfather's house.

I could talk to him about it.

He'd know how to make sense of it.

Grandpa Jonathan was the wisest man I'd ever known.

Nathan Laurent

THE WHISKEY BURNED my throat all the way down while the music soothed my soul.

My cousin, Isabella, played the piano like an angel. Probably one of the best things about being here with my cousins was listening to her music.

Even now, my younger brother and two of my cousins danced with girls who were supposed to be at the main house with their parents.

The Becquerels had invited several families over for a spring picnic and, since they had traveled some distance to get here, they had stayed overnight.

My cousins were a bit rowdy for my taste… ironic since I was from south Louisiana—with its reputation for breeding men with a wilder nature.

My family had come up from New Orleans for the summer —or however long it took—to get away from the yellow fever outbreak.

Unless a person had had the fever and lived to tell the tale, they were not welcome in polite society. It was one of those unwritten laws of New Orleans high society.

Since we had not had the misfortune of coming down with the fever, we would have been isolated.

It made little sense to me, this being shunned for being healthy. But it was the code we lived by, at least at the moment.

"Come," my oldest cousin Martin said, "Join our dance."

"And who exactly am I to dance with?"

"I'll dance with you," my cousin's girl said over her shoulder as they twirled past.

I didn't hear my cousin's response, but I noticed that he led her away, not stopping long enough to change dance partners.

It was well and good enough for me. I was content to watch. Not interested in being part of their illicit affairs.

Unfortunately, I was relegated to bunking here in my cousins' garçonnière for the duration of our stay here outside of Natchez.

I suppose I could have stayed in New Orleans. I was a grown man after all. But I needed to speak with my uncle Samuel about some business in the Natchez area. Besides, my brother, the oldest son, stayed behind to take care of the country house. Grant was content to be left to himself. The more alone time he had, the happier he was.

So we'd packed up. My parents, my sister, and my younger brother and traveled with a caravan of wagons and buggies north. It had taken us three days to get here.

After only being here a few days, the Becquerel family threw this picnic to introduce us to the locals.

If you asked me, it did nothing but incite trouble—the possibility of it anyway.

My younger brother was going to be in trouble before the month was out. I would bet money on it.

Needing to get some fresh air, I stepped outside into the early evening air. The moonlight glinted off the Mississippi River. The same river that passed alongside my father's property near New Orleans.

The water moved quicker than it looked. The river looked, and smelled, more like a putrid pond.

Tomorrow I would go into town. Do some initial research.

I wasn't one to put things off and since we'd been here for a few days, I was itching to get moving in a productive direction.

That's when I saw her.

Not more than six yards away. The profile of a beautiful siren with long brunette hair flowing around her shoulders. She stood there, looking out over the river, much as I did.

As the seconds became a minute, the girl turned her head and looked in my direction.

But her eyes didn't focus on me. Instead, she looked right through me. As though I wasn't even there.

I blinked and she was gone.

A shiver ran through me, but I shook it off.

A trick of the light, trying to distract me from following through with my plan.

I shook my head.

Not tonight.

Keep Reading WRITTEN IN THE WIND...

Kathryn Kaleigh writes sweet rom com, time travel romance, and historical romance.

kathrynkaleigh.com